Other books by Linda Mahkovec

The Dreams of Youth

Seven Tales of Love

The Garden House

The Christmastime Series

Christmastime 1940: A Love Story

Christmastime 1941: A Love Story

Christmastime 1942: A Love Story

Christmastime 1943: A Love Story

Christmastime 1944: A Love Story

D0111826

Christmastime 1939: Prequel to
the Christmastime series
by Linda Mahkovec
...
Copyright © 2018

Paperback: ISBN-13: 978-1-948543-69-9
ISBN-10: 1-948543-69-9
eBook: ISBN-13: 978-1-948543-70-5
ISBN-10: 1-948543-70-2

Distributed by Bublish, Inc.

Cover Design by Laura Duffy
©Tomoko K/Shutterstock.com

Christmastime 1939

Prequel to the Christmastime Series

LINDA MAHKOVEC

Chapter 1

◦∽

Home. Almost a week since Lillian Hapsey returned from her sister's house upstate, and things were exactly the same. The inspiration or revelation or solution she had hoped for hadn't happened. She hadn't thought her plans through. Instead, she had trusted that everything would fall into place, and now here it was – Christmas was almost upon her, and she had no Christmas spirit at all.

She let Tommy and Gabriel splash in the bathtub a little longer than usual. It gave her a chance to sort her thoughts, and to enjoy the hot water bottle on her lower back without the boys asking too many questions. She rested her feet on the small embroidered footstool and rubbed her legs.

A pile of clothing to be mended sat next to her, but she had no desire to get started on it. She frowned at her fatigue – it can't have anything to do with age, surely, she told herself. Thirty-four isn't exactly old. It must be the extra hours I've been putting in at work.

The small sketchbook she carried with her everywhere lay open on her lap. She paged through the drawings she had made from the visit to her sister's – rows of trees in the orchard with a few old apples and leaves clinging to the branches, her sister Annette knitting by the fireplace, a swing that hung from an old oak tree, another of Annette kissing her sleeping baby. Lillian's face softened at the memories. It had been a good trip.

She moved the hot water bottle to her lap and savored the stillness of the moment – a contrast to the busy week. It had begun with the train ride home from upstate, then back to her routine of scheduling babysitters for Tommy and Gabriel, and keeping up with her work at the department store. Now that Thanksgiving was behind them, the Christmas season had begun in earnest.

She leaned her head back against the couch and closed her eyes, wondering how she would muster up the energy and enthusiasm to get her through the season. The radiator rattled and whistled with coming steam. A soothing warmth began to fill the living room, chasing the cold away. She sank deeper into the couch, giving in to her weariness. The hissing and shshing of the radiator grew louder and louder, accompanied by the gurgling in the pipes. A peaceful oblivion overtook her.

After several minutes, the radiator sounds lowered to a sputter. Then a whisper. Then a soft, warm silence filled the small room. Broken by sounds of laughter and splashing from the boys.

Lillian opened her eyes and realized that she had dozed off. That won't do, she thought.

She sat up straight and looked about her. She couldn't help but compare her tiny Brooklyn apartment to her sister's rambling old house on the orchard with a lovely view out of every window – the flower beds and vegetable garden in the back that still showed a bit of color, the charming old cider house, the country road leading into town. From the upstairs bedroom window, the view was like stepping into a painting – softly undulating farmland dotted with red barns and white farmhouses, the orchard stretching out to the west, and in the distance, patches of woods and a small stream that sparkled in the sunlight.

And the sunsets! The golden light over the orchard swelled her heart each time she saw it. She often ran upstairs as the day was fading in order to catch it, making excuses as she suddenly left the room. "Just getting something from upstairs," or "I think I'll fetch my sweater." Not that she had to hide anything, she simply wanted those few minutes all to herself, to better take in the powerful stirring of beauty and longing. It was a reminder of girlhood dreams and all the things she was going to do with her life. She and Annette were raised in a town not far from the orchard and being upstate always plunged her into the past when she was young and full of dreams, before she and Annette had married and moved away.

Lillian shook away her thoughts and lifted a few items from the pile of clothes – three pairs of trousers, a few dresses, and a skirt.

"Tommy, Gabriel! Time to finish up!"

She threaded a needle and draped the first pair of trousers over her lap. Mrs. Harrison from the dry cleaner down the street was kind enough to throw a little business her way. It wasn't much, but it helped to supplement her earnings from the department store.

She pushed the needle through the woolen hem, trying to recapture the glimmer of Christmas excitement she had felt up at her sister's. A few days after Thanksgiving, Annette had begun to unpack some of her decorations. The children had caught her enthusiasm as they pulled out garlands and the crèche set and red ribbons.

Lillian smiled in memory of the afternoon they sat at the kitchen table with the children and prepared sliced oranges to dry for ornaments, and made clove and orange pomander balls. The scent of fresh citrus and cloves filled the kitchen while the kids sang Christmas songs and laughed when they made up the words they couldn't remember.

And the evening when they sat in front of the fire, the kids sprawled on the floor, cutting pictures out of the catalogs – until Annette's husband, Bernie, sent them all running and squealing when he crawled into the room growling and pawing like a bear.

Her smile deepened at the memory of rocking Annette's youngest, five-month-old Abigail.

Was there any greater sweetness than holding a baby as it smiled up at you and kicked its legs and shook its tiny fists in joy?

She set her sewing down. Is that what was making her sad? Knowing that she would never have another child? Or was it the nostalgia of being at Annette's? Or was she just tired?

Spending Thanksgiving this year with Annette and Bernie, rather than Christmas as she usually did, had seemed like a good idea at the time. But now Lillian felt a stab of dread at the mere thought of facing the Christmas holiday alone.

No need to fear Christmas, she thought, picking up her sewing again. She would simply follow Annette's advice, and start with their mother's Christmas recipes. That would put her in the holiday spirit. And then hang the stockings, and get a tree, and…

She glanced over at the time.

"Hurry up boys! Your show will be on soon."

The bathtub was soon gurgling as the plug was pulled and the water drained. She heard Tommy and Gabriel opening and shutting drawers as they pulled out their pajamas.

"Don't forget to brush your teeth!"

Lillian cast another glance at the living room. There wasn't a single sign of Christmas. She would have to get started.

Oddly enough, it would be their first Christmas together in Brooklyn. They had always celebrated the holiday upstate. Especially after Tom died, Annette had insisted that Lillian and the boys spend Christmas with her and Bernie and their growing family. With Tommy eight years old now, and Gabriel five, all their Christmas memories were from the orchard.

Lillian set her sewing down and brought the hot water bottle to the kitchen. This would be an important Christmas, and instead of preparing for it, she had spent these past few days filled with worry – missing Annette, hoping the landlord wouldn't raise the rent, and fretting about the new manager at work, Mr. Hinkley. He had never liked her, and when Mrs. Klein finally retired and he was promoted, he made his feelings abundantly clear. He still resented the older manager's preference for Lillian.

No need to ruin her evening thinking about him, she thought, sitting back down. The trip to Annette's was supposed to be a prelude to Christmas. But Lillian felt no surge of excitement. She wasn't in the mood for Christmas and would be glad when it was over. Everything felt wrong.

And of course, underlying everything, was the dark shadow cast by the war in Europe. The news reports grew more frightening with each passing day. She had believed that war would be averted. That Hitler would be appeased. But when he invaded Poland in the fall, England and France had declared war. Where would it all end?

She stared out and worried about a world controlled by Nazis and Fascists. Worried that the U.S. would be pulled into the war – or worse, that they would be attacked by Nazis. First bombed, then invaded, then…

"I'm finished!" cried Gabriel, running into the room. He jumped up on the couch next to her, clutching a wet teddy bear.

Lillian gave him a quick hug and then quickly pulled her sewing away from the dripping bear.

"Gabriel! You didn't give Taffy a bath again, did you?" She eyed the sodden teddy bear, and moved the pile of clothes to the coffee table.

"Just a little one."

"Go put him back in the bath tub until he dries out." She would deal with that later – wring out the bear and set him on top of the radiator to dry.

Tommy soon plopped down on her other side. "I told him not to, Mommy, but he didn't listen. This time he washed him with soap! Lots of soap."

"That's because he likes bubbles!" Gabriel hollered from the bathroom.

"He's not real!" Tommy shouted back.

Lillian sighed. "Hush, Tommy. I'll take care of it."

Gabriel was soon at her side again. "Mommy, does every word rhyme?"

She shifted her thoughts from the soapy teddy bear to his question, while keeping her eye on her sewing. "Most words rhyme with something," she said, amused by this latest word phase of his.

"What rhymes with Santa?" he asked.

"Let's see…" She looked out, trying to come up with something.

"What rhymes with Christmas?" asked Tommy.

She opened her mouth, but again drew a blank. "Hmm…"

Gabriel tugged on her sweater. "Who brings Santa *his* presents?"

Lillian dropped her sewing to her lap and suddenly felt tired. "I – I think his wife brings them."

"Oh." Then Gabriel sat up on his knees, in near panic. "Oh no! How will Santa find us this year? What if he brings our presents to Aunt Annette's?"

Tommy, who claimed not to believe in Santa Claus, nevertheless grew worried and waited for her answer.

"Well – when you write your letters to Santa," she replied, "you can tell him we're in Brooklyn this year. That way he'll know."

"Tonight?" asked Gabriel.

Lillian resumed sewing. "Maybe over the weekend, when we'll have more time."

"Or maybe never," Tommy grumbled. He didn't like the new plan of spending Christmas at home and had complained about it every day since returning.

Lillian hadn't expected him to be so upset over it. Had she made a big mistake in changing their plans?

Gabriel looked from Tommy to her. "Tommy said we're not having Christmas this year."

Lillian titled her head in reprimand to Tommy. "Not having Christmas? Now, how is that possible?"

She bit off the thread, and stuck the needle in the pin cushion. "Of course, we're going to have Christmas." She draped an arm around their shoulders and gave a light squeeze.

"How?" demanded Tommy.

"We'll figure that all out. It's still weeks away."

"You're just making excuses," said Tommy. "Like you did with the World's Fair. All summer you kept saying we could go, and then it was too late."

Lillian had intended to take them to the Fair but she had never found the time. And then it had shut down in October. "It will open again in the spring for another season. I promise we'll go next summer."

Tommy didn't look convinced.

She gazed at her boys, their hair still wet from their bath. Tommy's was neatly slicked over, but Gabriel's curls were already breaking free into soft waves. My God, but her heart ached with love for them. She looked at the flannel pajamas she had made them last year – red and white striped for Tommy, pale blue with a scatter of moons and stars for Gabriel. She noticed that the sleeves on Tommy's were well past his wrists. She would have to get busy if she was going to make them another set in time for Christmas.

She settled her eyes on Tommy. "You're growing so fast, Tommy."

"I'm growing so fast, too," said Gabriel, sitting tall.

"Yes, you are," she said.

"If we don't have Christmas with Aunt Annette and Uncle Bernie, what will we do?" asked Gabriel. "How else can we have Christmas?"

Again, she saw that Tommy was waiting for her answer. "First things first. Remember, you have your party at Dominic's tomorrow night."

"But that's for his birthday," said Gabriel. "Not Christmas."

Tommy crossed his arms. "Why did you say no to the firehouse party? We go there every Christmas. And then we go to Aunt Annette's. How come this year's different?"

Lillian rethreaded the needle. "Because I thought it would be nice to spend Thanksgiving with Annette, for a change. You loved it, Tommy. You and Gabriel spent all your time playing in the cider house and running around the orchard with your cousins."

"Yeah, but now we're back and we don't have any plans for Christmas! Not a single one." Tommy jumped to his feet and stood in front of her. "And you keep making excuses."

Gabriel also jumped up, planted himself next to Tommy, and folded his arms like him. "We want Christmas!"

Lillian made a few more stitches. "And we're going to have Christmas. You'll see. I thought it was time to start our own celebration, our own traditions."

"How?" asked Tommy, throwing out his arms. "You're never here, you're always working, you never have any time for us."

His words struck a tender spot. "This is the busiest time of year at the department store, Tommy. You know that. Besides, I have to work so that I can get you some nice presents."

"I thought Santa brings the presents," said Gabriel.

"He does. I – I meant school clothes and things for the house." She glanced over at the clock. "Look what time it is, boys!"

Tommy hurried to the radio and kneeled in front of it. "Come on, Gabe. Time to saddle up!" he cried, adjusting the knob. Gabriel sat cross-legged next to him.

The end of the news program came on, filling the small living room with words of gloom. "In more devastating news from China…"; "German Luftwaffe and U-boats continue to mine the estuaries of…"; "The destruction of yet another synagogue in the city of…"; "Britain increases the age range for conscription…"

Each phrase was a punch. Lillian's hands froze and her face twisted in worry. There was no doubt – it was getting worse and worse.

Tommy pointed his chin at the radio. "If I was a soldier, I'd send Hitler packing to the North Pole."

Gabriel's eyes widened. "You can't put Hitler with Santa!"

Tommy showed a slight sign of concern. "Then the South Pole."

Gabriel nodded his consent. "You think Santa will bring me a fire truck this year? And some Tinker Toys?"

"I'm going to ask for a Buck Rogers Pocket Pistol," said Tommy. "Even though I don't think there really is a Santa."

"That's okay, Tommy," said Gabriel. "Even if you don't believe in him, he still brings presents."

Tommy cast a sly glance to Lillian. "Then I'm also going to ask for a model airplane kit like Dom has and – " He snapped to attention as their program began. "Shhh!"

"I wasn't talking," said Gabriel, "you were!"

"Shhh!" Tommy said again. "Here they come."

Both boys lifted the imaginary reins to their horses and bobbed up and down as they rode alongside each other. Gabriel's smile widened at his pardner.

Lillian let out a deep breath, realizing that she had been holding it, tense with the news. Maybe she should have gone to Annette's for Christmas. It felt safer up there.

That was just an excuse, she thought. She had to follow through with her plans this year. Last Christmas she had made up her mind to spend Christmas here at home – but at the last minute she had fled to Annette's, afraid of being alone, of feeling the loss of Tom, afraid of the years ahead.

Lillian sat up straight. This year she would face Christmas on her own. Not with the help of her sister. Not with the help of Tom's friends from the firehouse. It had been four years since his death, and it was time to stand on her own.

While the boys listened to *The Lone Ranger*, Lillian completed hemming the trousers, and began to let out the seams on a dress. She tried to be clear-headed about her situation. She liked to believe that where there was a problem, there was also a solution.

First, she separated the problems that she had control over. She realized that most of them concerned money. She decided that if money was part of the problem, then it would also be part of the solution. She would try to pick up extra shifts when she could. And perhaps she could find a few more people who needed some sewing done.

Though what she really needed, as her friend Izzy was always pointing out, was to acquire skills that would enable her to work in an office. Perhaps she should think about taking a few classes some-where. Change would be good for her – yet she was afraid of making things worse. So, she did nothing.

When the radio program was over, Gabriel climbed onto the couch next to her and rested his head on her shoulder. "Mommy, do you have to go to work tomorrow? Can't you stay home? I don't want to go to the babysitter."

"Tomorrow is Saturday, the busiest shop-ping day. Especially with Christmas just around the corner." Saturday was the day the boys most complained about going to the babysitter's house, especially Tommy. During the week he was only there before and after school – but he was growing increasingly angry about Saturdays.

Tommy let out a groan.

"But I don't like Mrs. Peabody," said Gabriel. "She's crabby."

"Mrs. pea-brain," Tommy muttered, as he plopped down on the couch.

"Tommy!" chided Lillian.

"Mrs. peahen," Gabriel said softly, hoping to get away with his remark.

Tommy grinned and with a forward thrust of his head, imitated their babysitter. "Cluck, cluck!" he cried, sending him and Gabriel into peals of laughter.

"Boys, that's no way to speak about Mrs. Peabody. Besides, you don't like Mrs. Crawford either, or the Sisley sisters."

"That's because Mrs. Crawford sleeps all the time and talks to her birds all day long."

"Yeah," said Gabriel, "and she makes us eat lima beans. Yuck!"

"And we have to be quiet while the Sisley sisters teach piano," said Tommy.

Gabriel held up a finger. "But at least they give us cookies and milk."

"They give us digestive biscuits, Gabriel. Not cookies."

Lillian sighed. "I'll look for another sitter after the holidays."

Out of all the babysitters, Lillian much preferred the Sisley sisters, identical twins – who also dressed identically – Sylvia and Cynthia. They were two elderly spinsters of the old order, everything proper and correct. They taught piano lessons to the neighborhood children and were rarely available for babysitting. They were willing to help out in a pinch, provided it could be arranged well in advance, and provided that Tommy and Gabriel behaved themselves. The sisters had temporarily refused to babysit after discovering that Gabriel had been spinning their piano stool seats up and down, readjusting the heights right before a lesson. It had apparently thrown the sisters off for the rest of the day.

Tommy crossed his arms. "We should have stayed at Aunt Annette's for Christmas!"

"That's enough, Tommy. We were there for a whole week. You know I have to get back to work. And you have school."

"I know," Tommy said, his voice filled with resignation.

"We'll make this a very special Christmas," said Lillian.

Both boys looked up, willing to hope. "How?"

She put away her sewing materials and refolded the pile of clothes. The rest would have to wait. "We'll decorate our home with pine boughs. And get a Christmas tree, of course." There was no response. "We could make pomander balls."

"Nah. We already did that up at Aunt Annette's," said Tommy. He walked on his knees over to the bookshelf and lifted a book. He flipped through it, then closed it with snap and lifted a kaleidoscope to his eyes.

"Yeah, and the cloves hurt my fingers," said Gabriel. "They're sharp."

Lillian would be happy when Christmas was over. It was a wearisome puzzle she couldn't quite figure out.

"That's mine!" Gabriel cried, jumping up and snatching the kaleidoscope away from Tommy.

"You said I could have it," said Tommy, yanking it back.

"I changed my mind!"

A tug-of-war began that Lillian feared would result in a broken kaleidoscope. She got up and took the kaleidoscope away and set it on the bookshelf.

"Why are you two so fussy tonight?"

She spotted the book that Annette had tucked into the lunch basket, just as they were leaving for the train. She had forgotten all about it, and lifted it with a sense of being rescued.

"Look here!" she said, showing them the cover. "Annette said this will put us in the Christmas spirit. Come," she said, returning to the couch. "Let's begin it. It will be the start of our holiday celebration. We'll read a little bit each night. How about that?"

Gabriel was all for it and jumped onto the couch next to her. Tommy sat down on her other side and read the title. "About singing?"

"No. It's a story about a grouchy old man who hates Christmas. I read it many years ago." Lillian turned to the first page.

Tommy leaned over and read, "Stave One: Marley's Ghost." His eyes brightened and he sat up in anticipation.

Gabriel, never one for ghost stories, snuggled closer.

Lillian began to read. "Marley was dead, to begin with. There was no doubt whatever about that." She completed the first paragraph, reading, "Old Marley was as dead as a door-nail," and glanced at the boys, relieved to find them engaged.

Despite constant interruptions and questions – "Why is Scrooge so mean?" "Why does his nephew like him if he's so crabby?" "Why doesn't the clerk quit and find a different job?" "What rhymes with Scrooge?" – the boys enjoyed the tale and peered closer to examine the illustrations.

However, when Marley's face appeared on the door knocker, and when Scrooge thought he saw a hearse making its way up the stairs, and when all the bells began ringing in Scrooge's cavernous dark home, Gabriel buried his head in Lillian's arm. She placed her hand on him, assuring him that it was a happy tale. But when the ghost of Marley made his way up the stairs, rattling his chains, and then walked through the door, Gabriel covered his eyes.

"I don't like this story! I want to hear about Santy Claus."

"Scaredy cat!" said Tommy.

"I am not! I just don't like stories about dead ghosts!"

"Ghosts aren't real, Gabe."

"Then why is Scrooge so scared?" Gabriel asked.

"This part is almost over," said Lillian. She scanned the next line and saw that Marley untied the bandage around his head, causing his jaw to drop on his chest. She shut the book.

"All right," she said. "That's enough for tonight. I promise it gets happier." She kissed

Gabriel's forehead. "Time for bed. You can look at your picture book for five minutes."

"How about ten?" asked Tommy.

"All right. I'll tuck you in soon."

The boys raced to their room, and Lillian went to the kitchen to make her lunch for the next day. She opened the bread drawer and told herself that she just needed to get through the season. Then she would take stock and – and what? She didn't know what it was that she was waiting for.

Exhausted and dispirited, she kissed the boys goodnight, took a quick bath, and went to bed. She would read a few more pages of the tale by Dickens, so she would know which parts to skip for Gabriel. It was supposed to cheer them up, after all.

And yet, as she continued to read, she, too, felt disturbed by the simple story.

I read it as a girl, she thought. But I don't remember being so upset by Marley's ghost. Or was it the words he spoke to Scrooge? "I wear the chain I forged in life." And all those whirling, miserable spirits that filled the sky as Marley departed, howling and lamenting the time they wasted on Earth. Spirits of painful regret.

Once again, she realized how relieved she would be when the season was over. She quickly checked her thoughts – she sounded just like Scrooge, all grumpy and ill-tempered. Then appalled by the very thought, she denied it. She was nothing like Ebenezer Scrooge. Nothing at all like him. She was not mean and ungenerous and stingy. And she was happy, compared to him. Wasn't she? Yes, she wanted Christmas to be over, but that didn't make her in any way similar to Scrooge.

Scrooge's past had been sad and lonely. Hers was happy. In fact, hers was so happy that she was always trying to recreate it. Was she living too much in the past – missing her parents, and her girlhood days with Annette, and longing for the days of first love that would never come again?

Rather than dwell on those thoughts, she read on. She flipped ahead and saw the illustration of the Fezziwig's Christmas party, which she remembered as being a cheerful part of the story.

In a way, she had to admire the youthful Scrooge. In spite of his difficulties, he had mustered up his strength and made his way in the world, albeit with an underlying hardness.

She, on the other hand, had frittered away much of her youth. She had always been guided by her dreams, but they hadn't led to firm results. Maybe Mr. Scrooge was a better planner than she had been. But what a nasty man. And what a grouchy, miserly boss he was. Like Mr. Hinkley.

She decided to blame her lack of Christmas spirit on her job and Mr. Hinkley. She had argued with him before leaving for her visit upstate. He hadn't wanted her to take so much time off for Thanksgiving, but she explained that she had already planned her vacation, before he had been made manager. Still, she knew he disapproved of her in general and kept a watchful eye on her, waiting for her to make a mistake. She would need to be more careful.

She would begin anew tomorrow. Prove herself a good employee. She would wear her best suit, work harder, and make more sales for the department. And work late or extra hours if need be.

But the boys already complained that she was gone all the time. She needed this job, and couldn't risk losing it. She would make it up to the boys somehow, she thought, and once more lifted the book.

She read a few pages – only to realize that she had no idea what she had just read.

She lowered the book again and gazed out at her room. A picture of Tom by her bedside was the only evidence that he had once been there. No shirt or pants draped over the chair, no men's shoes sat at the closet door, as they used to. She smoothed her hand over the pillow next to her. Then she raised her head to the emptiness of the room, and spoke softly:

"Tom was dead. Of that there was no doubt."

Several hour-like minutes passed, and she closed the book. Then she turned off the lamp and curled on her side.

Poor old Scrooge. She couldn't get rid of the image of him returning home on Christmas Eve and eating gruel in his cold room. He was utterly miserable, but had only himself to blame.

She fluffed up her pillow and tucked her arm under her head. At least Scrooge didn't have to worry about money. The old miser. Pinching and scraping on coal and candles. At least he didn't have to worry about rent and bills, and –

A low creaking noise stopped her thoughts. She raised her head and listened. She cocked her head. Nothing. She sank back into her pillow.

She shouldn't have read a ghost story to the boys right before sleeping. She hoped they wouldn't have nightmares about clanking chains and footsteps in the night and –

There it was again! She lifted her head and peered at the open doorway. Ridiculous! Perhaps she was more like Scrooge than she cared to admit. She pulled up the blanket and settled in once more.

What was Annette thinking, giving me this book to cheer me up? Noises in the dark. Ghosts and hearses and bells ringing of their own accord. How is that supposed to get me in the Christmas spirit? It's left me in an impressionable state of mind. She peered again at her doorway, half expecting Marley to come floating in. Was she like Scrooge? What was she so afraid of?

She would look for a happy book about Christmas. Gabriel was right. She would find a story about Santa and elves and –

Again! A small rustling sound. She was sure. She lifted her head, and turned her face to the left, the right, straining to make it out. Slowly, she pushed herself up, pulled the blanket up to her chin, and remained absolutely motionless.

There was an unmistakable noise near her bed, coming towards her. A crawling, scraping sound – and breathing? Yes! Her heart pounded in unreasonable fear.

She would have to turn on the lamp or lie there terrified. She must do it!

She forced herself to reach over, and quickly snapped on the lamp – just as Tommy and Gabriel jumped from their crouching position at the foot of her bed.

"Booo!" they cried, laughing and scrambling onto her bed. She caught a flash of red and blue pajamas before they dove under the blanket and nestled next to her.

Lillian placed her hand over her heart. "What is going on! Scaring me like that! Why aren't you boys in bed?" she asked, never so happy to see their smiling little faces.

"Gabriel's scared of ghosts," said Tommy.

"So are you!"

"No, I'm not." Tommy propped himself up on his elbow.

"Mommy, can we sleep with you tonight?" asked Gabriel. "Please?"

The look of sternness fell from her face and both boys snuggled closer. She wrapped her arms around them, nuzzling their faces. Little bundles of love and joy tucked safely into her arms.

"All right. Just for tonight."

Chapter 2

Lillian awoke early the next morning, slipped on a housedress, and ran downstairs to the milk box to pick up the fresh bottles and return the empties. Though the dawn had broken, heavy skies cast the world in gray. She paused a moment on the stoop to listen to the sounds of Brooklyn – the early rumbling of trains and the clang of the trolleys a few blocks over. The various caws and coos from seagulls, pigeons, and blackbirds. And from the nearby basement, the scraping of iron against cement as the super shoveled coal into the burner.

She rubbed her arms against the cold, picked up the fresh bottles of milk, and hurried back upstairs to make breakfast for Tommy and Gabriel.

She boiled a few eggs and set the bread and butter on the table. Annette's apple butter and peach preserves would add a nice touch. She roused the boys and set out their clothes, and then went to her room to dress for work.

Foremost in her mind was the thought that she would make this a good Christmas for Tommy and Gabriel. Every problem had a solution, and she would set about solving hers instead of being overwhelmed by them. Problem. Solution. It was simple.

To begin with, she thought, looking through her closet at her best pieces, she would stop worrying about Mr. Hinkley. She had a loyal clientele, which Mr. Hinkley was aware of, and she knew the dress salon as well as, if not better than, he. She had the advantage of being able to speak freely to her customers about which styles worked with their figures, in a manner that Mr. Hinkley could not.

She decided to wear her best suit – the gray Merino wool with a black velvet collar. She wore her pearl earrings and pinned a Christmas brooch at the neck of her white blouse – a swirl of green mistletoe set with seed pearls. She applied a touch of lipstick, checked her reflection, and then looked in on the boys. Tommy could dress himself, but Gabriel still needed help with buttons. Soon they were all dressed and sitting at the kitchen table.

Lillian prepared a cup of tea for herself, while listening to Tommy and Gabriel discuss their outing with Dom, Tony, and little Mary Rossi – their best friends who lived one street behind them.

As she feared, the boys' enthusiasm dwindled as they left their apartment and began to walk the six blocks to the babysitter's apartment building. The closer they got, the more they grumbled.

"A whole day with Mrs. Peabody!" said Tommy, wrinkling up his face.

"It will go by in a flash," Lillian said cheerfully. "And then you have your night at Dom's house. Won't that be fun? We'll have to reciprocate for your birthday, Tommy." The smile she hoped to elicit from Tommy didn't materialize.

They walked the last block in silence, Tommy slapping at anything in his path – an ash can, a wrought iron fence, a lamppost. Gabriel kicked at a wadded up paper bag, and the side of the same lamppost Tommy had smacked.

They entered the babysitter's brownstone and climbed the two flights to her floor, Tommy and Gabriel dragging their feet. Lillian stopped suddenly when she saw the babysitter waiting in her doorway with her arms crossed, as if she was already angry at the boys.

"Good morning, Mrs. Peabody. Are we late?" asked Lillian. "Tommy, Gabriel, hurry up! Mrs. Peabody has been waiting for us." They climbed the last flight and Lillian gathered the boys in front of her.

Mrs. Peabody's stance remained unchanged. She towered over the boys in the doorway and cast a disapproving glance at them. A "hmph!" shot from her face and landed on the two upturned faces.

Tommy pushed Gabriel in front of him, landing him inches away from Mrs. Peabody's apron that was always covered with cooking smears. Gabriel's face wrinkled up and he stepped back. "I don't want to stay here!"

"Shh! Gabriel!" Lillian widened her eyes at him. "Is everything all right, Mrs. Peabody?"

"No, everything is *not* all right, and never will be again!"

Lillian waited for an explanation but soon realized that she was meant to ask about the bad news.

"Is something wrong? Has something happened?" she asked, genuinely concerned, but at the same time hoping the explanation wouldn't make her late for work.

"What has happened, as you say, is that cousin Jedediah took sick in the night. And has expired." Her head, in a very peahen-like manner, Lillian couldn't help but think, pecked from her, to Tommy, to Gabriel, and back to her, empty beaked. "Passed!"

Though Lillian's brow was now creased, Mrs. Peabody jerked her head back at the paltry response to her tragic news.

"Oh! I'm so sorry," said Lillian. In the five months she had been taking the boys to Mrs. Peabody's, Lillian had heard her speak – on numerous occasions – of troublesome neighbors, dishonest storekeepers, and difficult relatives. But she had never heard of cousin Jedediah.

Tommy cocked his head up to the babysitter. "You mean he's dead?"

Mrs. Peabody gave a quick gasp. "Indeed, he is!"

"Dead as a door-nail?" Gabriel asked. "Like Jacob Marley?"

Mrs. Peabody's mouth and eyes opened wide and her chest puffed up. She grabbed the doorway for support.

Just as Lillian was about to explain, Tommy asked, "Or as dead as a coffin nail?" pleased that he, too, remembered the exact words from Dickens.

"Oh, you wicked, wicked boys! I will not have cousin Jedediah's memory sullied." She sniffled and raised her apron to her nose. "Yes, he drank too much and never could hold down a job. And he never paid me back the $21.00 I gave him from my hard-earned savings. That was five years ago! The low-down, good-for-nothing rascal," she muttered to herself. "But he was my cousin, all the same. And he's gone! Not to be made light of by urchins like you."

"They don't know what they're saying." Lillian mistakenly thought a small laugh would soften the situation. "You see, I was reading *A Christmas Carol* to them last night and – "

"What do I care what you're reading!" cried Mrs. Peabody. "Cousin Jedediah is dead, and this is going to be a terrible, terrible Christmas. Worse than usual."

Tommy and Gabriel exchanged a glance. "Bah!" Tommy said in a low voice.

"Humbug!" Gabriel added.

"Well!" Mrs. Peabody folded her arms across her smudgy apron. "For my part, I have never come across such disrespectful creatures in all my life! Making a joke of cousin Jedediah's departure." She lifted her apron to her dry eyes, leaving a smear of butter on her glasses. She pecked her head back and then forward to determine why her vision had suddenly blurred, causing her to look cross-eyed at her lenses.

Tommy and Gabriel used both hands to cover their mouths, but their laughter still wriggled out.

"I will *not* put up with this. Off with you!" Mrs. Peabody dropped her apron and used it to shoo the boys away. She planted her hands on her hips. "And you, Miss Happy-All-the-Time Hapsey, can just find yourself another sitter!" She slammed the door in their faces.

"Good!" said Tommy. "She's always crabby and I hate her."

"Me too," echoed Gabriel. "She smells like cabbage!"

"Shh!" Lillian said sharply, waiting to see if the door would reopen. When it didn't she bit her lip, and headed down the stairs. "Let's go."

Tommy tossed an angry glare over his shoulder, and cried "Bah humbug!" as a parting good-riddance remark.

Gabriel scowled at the closed door, fists on his hips. "Yeah! Bah humbug bah humbug bah humbug!" He then hurried down the stairs in case the door should suddenly open. Tommy burst into laughter and tried to overtake him.

"Tommy! Gabriel! Behave yourselves! What's gotten into you two?" She turned to them with a flash of anger and continued down the stairs as they ran past her. "You know better than to mock someone about a death."

When she reached the first floor, she opened the vestibule door and fixed the boys with a look of reprimand. They fell silent, their small faces filled with a mix of guilt and justification. Lillian walked ahead of them on the sidewalk, furious at the way the morning was turning out.

She stopped suddenly, causing Tommy and Gabriel to bump into her. They all looked at each other in a *Now What?* moment.

She took their hands and began walking briskly back home. She knew that her emergency babysitter, the elderly Mrs. Crawford on the first floor, was with her sister for a few days. And the Sisley sisters had to be scheduled at least a week in advance – if there was one thing that flustered them it was a last-minute request. She closed her eyes, and let out a soft groan at the telephone call she would have to make. This was just the sort of thing Mr. Hinkley would use against her.

She stepped into a café, positioned the boys near the telephone booth, and held up her finger to them in warning.

"Not a word out of either of you!"

She entered the booth and closed the door behind her. Then she took a coin from her purse, gathered her thoughts, and placed the call to Mr. Hinkley. Her voice was full of apology as she explained that she would not be in to work today.

"Yes, I know I just returned from vacation, but the babysitter canceled…Yes, I understand it's the Christmas season." She held out the receiver, indignant at the volley of criticism pouring out of it. "I can make up the day, any day, just say when." She nodded, trying to get a word in. "I – yes – I realize that, Mr. Hinkley, and I'm sorry. But – " A loud click cut her short.

She stared at the receiver, and placed it back on the hook. She stared down at the floor, a sense of defeat beginning to overwhelm her. Then her temper shot up. "I'll find another job if it comes to that," she said aloud, exiting the telephone booth.

Tommy started to crack his knuckles. "What'd he say?"

"I've been warned. One more time, and I'm fired."

"Sorry, Mommy," said Tommy.

Gabriel directed his anger at the phone booth. "Bah Humbug!" he yelled, and kicked it for good measure.

Lillian took his arm. "That's enough, Gabriel! Let's go home."

Outside, she glanced up at the sky that had grown darker, threatening rain. She picked up her pace.

They walked in silence for two blocks, Lillian's mind on a list of things that must be done immediately – a new babysitter, more sewing from Mrs. Harrison, and, possibly, a new job.

She stopped to buy a newspaper to scan the help wanted ads. When they passed the German bakery, Tommy and Gabriel broke free to look wide-eyed at the freshly baked cupcakes being set in the window.

"Look, Tommy! Cupcakes with Christmas trees!" cried Gabriel.

Tommy and Gabriel watched as the baker's wife set a platter of cupcakes in the widow – the swirled buttercream frosting was decorated with green sugared Christmas trees dotted with red.

The baker's wife smiled at the boys. Lillian stopped and looked in the window, then down at the two hopeful faces now lifted to her in silent pleading.

She lifted her finger to them in a scolding manner. "You are *not* being rewarded for bad behavior, do you understand?"

They bobbed their heads up and down, with big smiles.

She opened the door to the bakery, the small bell tinkling in greeting. "But a little treat can't hurt."

Christmastime 1939

Chapter 3

As they left the bakery, a few sprinkles of cold rain began to fall. Tommy and Gabriel raised their faces to the sky and tried to catch raindrops with their tongues, while Lillian held the newspaper above her head and clutched the bakery box close to her. They quickened their pace as the rain began to fall more heavily, running the last block. They dashed up the steps to their brownstone and ducked into the vestibule.

"Are the cupcakes safe?" asked Gabriel.

Lillian inspected the box. "Not a drop on them."

Tommy and Gabriel sprinted up the stairs, the day turning out unexpectedly well for them. Lillian unlocked the door, and the boys kicked off their shoes and wriggled out of their wet coats. They hurried to the table, eyes wide in anticipation. Gabriel pulled out a chair and tucked his legs beneath him, while Tommy reached for two small plates and placed them in front of him and Gabriel.

Lillian set the bakery box on the kitchen table. "How about a glass of milk to go with your cupcakes?" As she poured two glasses of milk, the boys lifted their cupcakes out of the box and positioned them in the middle of their plates.

"I'm going to start at the top of the tree," said Gabriel, turning his cupcake around.

"I'm starting at the bottom," said Tommy.

Lillian smiled, thinking how easy it was to make them happy. She believed that happiness was the natural state for children, and that if she could simply protect and encourage it, the result would be joyful children. But it was not always so easy to achieve, she thought, fretting over the day's lost salary. She unfolded the newspaper on the other end of the table and spread the pages to dry, and then went to her bedroom to change out of her suit.

A few minutes later, she lit the burner to boil water for a cup of coffee. It would help to fortify herself for the task ahead. After finishing their cupcakes, Tommy and Gabriel sprawled out on the living room floor. Gabriel laid out pieces from Tommy's Lincoln Logs to build a cabin. Tommy lined up his tin soldiers for battle.

Though her intention was to look for a job, the headlines pulled her in a different direction. The Nazis raiding the Jewish Quarter in Krakow, Poland. The Soviets moving closer to the Mannerheim Line and Finland appealing to the League of Nations for intervention – would anyone help these people?

After reading for half an hour, she pushed the paper away in fear and disgust. The world was changing, even here in America. She could sense it in a thousand little ways. There was a clear shift towards meanness and intolerance. The German American Bund was growing in strength. Hatred was being stirred up and fueled by vile rhetoric.

She used to believe the acts of aggression were the result of the lean and difficult years of the '30s here and in other parts of the world. But now she feared that something else was at work. Tensions that had simmered for years had erupted into all-out war, following the German invasion of Czechoslovakia, and the partition of Poland by the Nazis and the Soviets. The Soviets were now in Finland, and the Japanese in China. Good God, where would it all end? There was talk that Hitler would take one country after another, but surely that would never happen.

She used to argue about it with her friend Izzy and held the position that it was the culmination of a period of resentment that would soon burn itself out. They had countless discussions. Last year Lillian had insisted that Hitler's own people, among the most cultured in the world, would stand up to him. Like most Americans, she had favored isolationism.

Izzy had argued that a terrible madness was seizing the world. She believed that Hitler must be stopped at all costs and declared that she would go herself if she were allowed to fight.

Lillian had believed that the world would come to its senses and turn its back on the delusional, hate-filled aggressors. But the past months had proved Izzy right. Lillian had a sinking feeling that evil had been let loose in the world and was gaining momentum.

She was suddenly frightened. Frightened by the world at large, by human nature. She was frightened at what was coming, and feared that she didn't have the wherewithal to take care of herself and her boys. The swirling pool of fears began to churn, eddying them up to the surface – fears of war, as well as concerns closer to home.

Her immediate fear was that she would lose her job. She didn't trust Mr. Hinkley. And perhaps she had been foolish, believing in her own importance to the department. She had lost several days' pay while at Annette's, and now today. What if more days were to follow?

Four years had not made her any better at being alone. She was not like other people. She was not like Izzy, charging through life in full control and enjoying every minute of it. Or like her sister, Annette, taking pleasure in every day.

Lillian was at a crossroads and didn't know which direction to take. And so she stood there in the middle of the road doing nothing, wringing her hands, while life passed her by.

She raised her eyes to the gray sky outside the rain-streaked window. Here she was, in her thirties, a widow, living in Brooklyn, far from her girlhood home upstate. Again, she considered moving back there. But what would she do? How would she support herself? Once more, she decided against it. At least she could always find work here in New York City. She sat up straight, took a sip of coffee, and placed the newspaper squarely in front of her.

She turned to the help wanted section, and lifted her pencil, in earnest about her job search. But the more she looked, the more discouraged she became. For the most part, the only jobs listed for women were for domestic help: *Baby Maids, Cooks, Houseworkers, Nursemaids, General housework.* The ads for sales were all for men: *Sales Help Males, Aggressive Salesman.*

She lay her pencil down, disheartened at not seeing a single sales clerk position for women. Of course, the department stores had already done their hiring for the Christmas season – she should have known that.

Her brow furrowed. She *must* keep her job. It was so much better than anything else offered in the newspaper. She rose to her feet and stood at the window. Through the rivulets of rain on the glass, she looked down at the street below. A car drove by, splashing water onto the curb. A few people hurried along the sidewalk, huddled under black umbrellas. Across the way, a few lights showed in the brownstone windows. But for the most part, the day was cold, still, and gray.

"Mommy?" Gabriel came into the kitchen. "What are you looking at?"

"Hmm?" Lillian lifted him to her hip. "Just the rain. It will be a good night for you boys to see a film with Dom and Tony."

"And Mary," he added.

"And little Mary." She kissed his warm cheek and set him down. He ran back to play with Tommy.

By late morning, her head ached and her notepad remained largely blank, except for a few jobs she had written down and then crossed out. She eyed the sketches she had made in the margins of the notebook – a small village with a rainbow, a gate leading to a garden, a fairytale tower.

She dumped her cold coffee in the sink and considered making a fresh cup. She glanced over at Tommy and Gabriel. They were now reading comic books on the couch, with a quilt shared between them. They had played nicely together all morning, but now they were getting bored and growing argumentative, pulling at the cover.

"You have more than half!" said Gabriel, with a tug at the quilt.

"That's because I'm bigger than you and need more." Tommy yanked the cover towards him.

Lillian sat back down at the table and looked at her list of possible jobs. She dreaded filling out applications, hoping to be hired. She added a little bench to the flower garden, then drew a birdbath with a small splashing bird.

"Fine! Take it." Tommy kicked the quilt off his legs, slid off the couch, and tossed his comic book to the floor.

"I want to go see if Dom can play. Can I?"

"Not now, Tommy. I told his mother I would bring you and Gabriel over at six o'clock. It's enough that you'll be seeing a movie and spending the night with them. You don't need to be there all day."

"But I want to go outside."

"Me too," said Gabriel. "Please, Mommy?"

"It's raining…" Lillian let the sentence fade.

But after another half hour, they were at it again. "Can we go outside *now*?" demanded Tommy.

"I'm hungry, Mommy!" said Gabriel.

Lillian pushed aside the newspaper and glanced at the clock. "I didn't realize how late it was. Let me fix you some lunch." She scooted back her chair and rubbed her neck. "Tommy, will you check the mail for me?"

He went down the stairs, happy to have something to do. Lillian opened the breadbox and took out a half loaf of bread. Peanut butter and jelly sandwiches would have to do, and a can of soup. When she opened the cupboard she saw that they were out of soup.

Tommy soon came running back up the stairs. He entered the apartment, his face filled with happiness. "Mommy, look who's here! Miss Briggs!"

Lillian spun around. "Izzy!" She closed the cupboard, and went to greet her friend. "Come in. Let me take your umbrella."

"Hi, Miss Briggs!" cried Gabriel, running up to Izzy.

"Miss Briggs?" Izzy asked, playfully indignant. She tousled his hair. "I'm Izzy to you two."

"What a nice surprise!" said Lillian. It was as if a burst of summer sunshine entered the apartment.

"My sis and her husband are up for the weekend. They're over at Aunt Ethel's now. I left them there to visit, and thought while I'm in Brooklyn I'd pop in the department store for a little early Christmas shopping. I stopped by to see you, but they told me you weren't working today. I thought you worked every Saturday."

"Babysitter problems. I had to call off work today and Mr. Hinkley was not happy about it. I wouldn't be surprised if he fires me. So," Lillian pointed to the newspaper and her notebook, "I've been checking out the want ads. How about a cup of coffee?"

Izzy caught the worry in her friend's voice. "I have a better idea. How about lunch?" She turned to Tommy and Gabriel. "You boys hungry?"

"Starving!" said Tommy with a wide smile. Gabriel began to jump up and down at the possible outing.

"Me too," said Izzy. "Let's go grab a bite. My treat."

"Oh Izzy, you don't have to do that," said Lillian.

"Please, you'll be doing me a favor. I just couldn't eat Aunt Ethel's stew again, and as a result I'm famished. Let's go to Saporito's – nobody has better minestrone soup. And their meatball sandwich..." Izzy rolled her eyes at the thought.

"Just give me a minute, Izzy." Lillian hurried to her bedroom to change out of her housedress.

Izzy smiled at Tommy and Gabriel who were already pulling on their shoes and coats.

"I don't know," she said, rubbing her chin. "What do you think – too cold for an ice cream sundae?"

The boys' eyes grew wide and they shook their heads. "I'm not cold," said Gabriel.

"Because that sure sounds good to me," said Izzy. She inspected the bruise on Tommy's cheek. "Where'd you get that shiner?"

Tommy gave a lopsided grin. "Playing Johnny-on-the-pony. When Hersh jumped up on us, we all fell down."

"No wonder. He's that big fella, isn't he?" Izzy screwed her eyes at Gabriel's shoes. "Wrong way." She knelt down and while Gabriel leaned on her shoulders to balance himself, she switched his shoes. "There we go!" She helped him to button his coat.

From the bedroom Lillian heard Tommy and Izzy discussing various street games. Izzy, who had spent part of her youth in Brooklyn, knew all the games and rules. Lillian overheard them talking about the ins and outs of skelly, a game she had never quite figured out.

Lillian dabbed on a bit of lipstick. She had to admit that Izzy's unexpected visit lifted her right out of the doldrums. Izzy – always beautifully dressed, always happy and determined, always up for fun, and full of good ideas. Everyone should have a friend like Izzy, she thought.

Tommy handed Izzy her umbrella, gave Lillian hers, and lifted a smaller umbrella from the stand. "Me and Gabe will share."

They were soon making their way to Saporito's through rain that was coming down hard. Lillian and Izzy huddled close together but were still pelted by the slanting rain. Tommy pointed his umbrella before him like a shield, raised an imaginary sword, and thrust it at the foe. "Arrgh!"

Gabriel howled with delight, and wheeled his arms around. "I'm swimming!"

"They've got the right attitude," laughed Izzy. "Taking on the storm with gusto! Come on – let's run!"

A few minutes later, they stumbled into Saporito's, all laughing and their cheeks pink from the exertion and cold. They shook out their umbrellas, and Lillian and Izzy took handkerchiefs from their purses and blotted their faces dry.

Soon they were all seated in a booth, enjoying the warmth and aromas filling the café – simmering garlic and onions and herbs. As usual, a scratchy Italian aria filled the air, accompanied by Mr. Saporito's humming behind the counter.

They read the specials on the chalkboard and placed their orders. "Egg creams all round?" asked Izzy.

Tommy and Gabriel hesitated.

Lillian smiled. "You can have one, boys." But they still looked as if they were debating the choice.

"Don't worry," said Izzy. "You can still have dessert afterwards," which set them wiggling and fidgeting in excitement. They exchanged glances at their sudden stroke of good luck, and Tommy draped his arm around Gabriel.

While the boys eyed the desserts in the glass case, debating between cake and the list of ice cream choices on the board behind the counter, Izzy asked Lillian what had happened at work.

After Lillian recounted the string of grievances Mr. Hinkley had against her, Izzy gently pressed her about what she would do if she lost her job. Lillian took a sip of her egg cream and then lifted and dropped her shoulders. "Find another one."

Izzy leaned back when their plates arrived and nodded in approval as Tommy and Gabriel bit into their sandwiches as if they hadn't eaten in days.

"I think a change is all you need. I know you get tired of me saying it, but I wish you'd consider moving to Manhattan. You'd love it! I can see you there, working at a new job, living in a new neighborhood, maybe taking a few art classes."

Izzy was one of the few people Lillian had shared her dreams about pursuing her art studies. A soft glow suffused Lillian's face and her eyes brightened at the vision. "It sounds like a dream." She looked out the window at the traffic and pedestrians, and gave a deep sigh. "Maybe someday." She noted Izzy's disappointment. "I'll think about it. I will. At the moment, I just need to get through the season."

Izzy nodded. "You boys all ready for Christmas?"

Tommy gave a snort of complaint. "We don't even have a tree yet."

"No tree?" She turned to Lillian as if shocked.

"Well, not yet," Lillian said. "Perhaps next week ..."

"And we have to write our letters to Santa," added Gabriel. "To tell him we're in Brooklyn this Christmas."

Lillian felt a stab of guilt. "Next week. I promise. We'll decorate our apartment, and you can write your letters to Santa."

Izzy took a long sip of her chocolate egg cream. "What's the date for the firemen's Christmas party?"

"Mom says we can't go," grumbled Tommy. He ate the last of his sandwich and pulled on the straw to his egg cream, making a loud slurping sound.

"No?" Izzy raised her eyebrows to Lillian.

Lillian dipped a slice of buttered bread into the last of her rigatoni. "I – I decided against it this year." She tried to sound cheerful.

The waiter stopped by and offered coffee to Lillian and Izzy. "Yes, thank you," Lillian said, again in a cheery tone that caused Izzy to look more closely at her.

"Hey!" Tommy suddenly spotted his friend Vinnie in the back and gave a big wave. "Can I go say hi?"

"Me too?" asked Gabriel.

"All right, but make it quick." Lillian waited until the boys had scrambled out of the booth, and then answered Izzy's questioning eyes.

"It's time I face Christmas on my own – without help from Annette or Tom's friends at the firehouse. They're a wonderful group. Kinder, more generous men couldn't be found. They brought us a tree every year since Tom's death, and always invite us to their gatherings. But this year I declined their help. I told them I had other plans."

"I'm sure they'd love to help you."

"They have their own growing families. And there are more recent widows who need their assistance. It's been four years. I'll always be grateful for their support, and for the love and respect they had for Tom, but…"

"I understand. You're afraid of being a burden to them. I'm sure they don't see it that way."

Lillian let out a sigh. "I guess I just to need to show everyone – including myself – that I can manage on my own. I've let myself be dependent on others for too long. Annette still worries about me. She encouraged me over Thanksgiving to believe in myself and to be strong – then reassured me that I can always move back upstate. I think she's hoping I'll marry someone up there so that she can keep an eye on me." She stirred some sugar into her coffee and added a splash of milk.

"Any chance of that?" asked Izzy.

"No. I'll never marry again." Lillian looked into her coffee and then took a sip. "This is my home now. At least I can always find work here." She kept to herself the fact that everything up there reminded her of loss. Tom. Her parents. The past.

Izzy nodded, but remained silent.

"If I moved back, I would backslide," Lillian added. She blamed herself for her weakness, for being too dreamy. She had always let her parents and Annette, and later, Tom, make the hard decisions while she drew and painted and took long walks with her head in the clouds. She sat up straight. "No. This year I'm determined to stand on my own."

"So, you're going to face it head on. Good for you! And your sister's right. You are strong, and you'll be just fine."

Tommy and Gabriel returned just as the waiter was clearing the table. They placed their orders for dessert, and were soon digging into chocolate sundaes with whipped cream.

"A little training and you could land yourself a good job," Izzy said, continuing her train of thought. She had ordered peppermint ice cream and savored the first bite. "Why don't we meet for lunch one day, and let me show you around Rockwell Publishing. Just to give you an idea of what's out there."

"Mom won't do it," said Tommy, his mouth full of ice cream. "She likes to say no to everything. *No* to Aunt Annette's for Christmas. *No* to the fire-house party. *No* to everything."

Lillian opened her mouth in surprise. "What are you talking about? We just returned from Annette's! And tell Izzy what you boys are going to do tonight."

Gabriel sat up on his knees. "It's Dom's birthday! We're spending the night at his house and his mom and dad are taking us to see *The Wizard of Oz.*"

"It's in Technicolor," added Tommy with importance.

"And eat popcorn. And then we're going to stay up late and sleep on the living room floor. Like camping."

Izzy's face shone with delight. "What fun!" She leaned back and turned to Lillian as if she had caught her at something. "Soooo, that means you're free tonight?"

"Well, I … "

Izzy wagged her finger. "No excuses! You're coming out with me. I'm taking Lois and Sonny to hear some music with a few friends. Drinks, dancing, a few laughs – and you're coming with us! Lois and Sonny are going into the city early, but they can give you a ride back to Brooklyn on their way back to Aunt Ethel's."

"Oh, I don't know … "

"Mom won't go," Tommy interrupted. "I told you, she says no to everything."

"That's not true," Lillian said. Then she wondered if there was any basis to his claim.

"Yes, it is," Tommy insisted.

Izzy put a fist on her hip, playfully outraged. "Do you say *no* to everything?"

"No!" said Lillian. "No."

"No, no," echoed Tommy.

Gabriel burst out laughing. "No, no, no, no, no!"

Izzy smiled at Lillian. "So, you'll join us tonight?"

Lillian looked from Gabriel to Tommy, both with their eyebrows raised waiting for her answer.

"I'd love to."

Christmastime 1939

Chapter 4

Being with Izzy was always like a tonic. The lunch had lifted Lillian's spirits, dispelling any sense of gloom, and Tommy and Gabriel stayed in high spirits for the entire afternoon. In the early evening, Lillian dropped the boys off at the Rossi's apartment, and went home to dress for her night out, surprised by how much she was looking forward to it.

From the back of her closet, she looked at her few good dresses, and decided on the simple black velvet with sheer polka dot netting around the neck and shoulders. It would be a nice change to be around a happy gathering, with dancing, music, and conversation. And how lovely it would be to see Lois and Sonny again. She had met them a few times and they were always good company.

As Lillian put on her lipstick and her pearl clip earrings, she tried to remember the last time she had gone out. There had been weddings and gatherings with the firemen's families. But a dance? It had been years.

Izzy had invited her out many times, but Lillian always declined. She now paused to ask herself if there was some truth to Tommy's assertion that it was her habit to say no to everything. Of course, she would have declined had Izzy not been between beaus. Tonight, there would be no awkwardness in being a single person among couples.

Izzy never had a shortage of admirers, and it was rare that she wasn't keeping company with some man. But her affairs never lasted long, and Lillian had the impression that Izzy could take them or leave them. Izzy could be exacting and would settle for nothing less than her ideal.

And yet she always enjoyed herself, and loved dancing, loved bringing people together, and meeting new people. She was always the life of the party, infusing any gathering with a sense of fun and sparkle. Lillian had once asked her if she thought she would eventually find the right man, and Izzy had merely shrugged off the matter. "Either I'll find him, or I won't. Either way, I'm going to have myself a good time." And she would, Lillian thought.

Lillian rode the subway into Manhattan and soon found the nightclub. After checking her coat, she looked out over the dance floor and spotted Izzy at a table with several other people.

Lillian made her way along the edge of the dance floor, and as she approached the table, she noticed that, as usual, Izzy was in the middle of all the action. She was telling some story that set them all laughing. Lillian noticed that several men from the nearby tables watched her with amusement, and desire, drawn by Izzy's effervescence. Izzy was used to such attentions, and didn't seem to notice.

There sat Izzy, dazzling as usual. She wore a light green satin dress that set off her auburn hair, and deeper green-gold crystals adorned her ears, neck, and wrist. Her quick movements and sudden bursts of laughter caused the faceted crystals to glint and sparkle – as if an inner fire burned within her and flashed out through her jewelry.

Izzy jumped up to greet Lillian and made room for her, introducing her to her friends. Lois and Sonny, great dancers, were on the floor and waved to her. Within minutes, Lillian had a cocktail in hand and was joining in the lively conversation.

"Lois and Sonny have been dancing since they arrived. They're living it up before returning to Baltimore tomorrow. It's been great having them here."

There were a few couples at their table, and several single people, all friends of Izzy's. Some of them took to the dance floor, while others kept to the table in conversation. Lillian danced a few dances, and seeing that Lois and Sonny had returned to the table, she sat back down to join them.

Lois greeted her with a hug. "I told Sonny I needed a break," she said. "He's tireless and could dance all night, but as I pointed out to him, he has the advantage of flat shoes." She leaned back into Sonny, who wrapped his arms around her.

Lillian asked about their children, and Lois explained that Sonny's parents were watching them for the weekend. "It's good for all of us to have some time apart. Though, I have to say, I can't wait to get back to them."

"I know what you mean. Tommy and Gabriel are spending the night at a friend's house, and it will feel so strange not to have them at home."

Sonny was soon in an animated discussion about boxing with the man at the next table, which eventually led to recounting the previous year's victory of Joe Lewis over the German Max Schmeling. The match had been seen as a triumph over Hitler and his claims of Aryan superiority. Predictably, the conversation turned to the war in Europe. Lillian, unable to make up her mind about the correct course of action for the U.S. – and in need of a night of merriment – was glad to have Izzy and Lois there to talk about other things.

They were soon discussing their plans for Christmas, and began to compare holiday recipes. Though Izzy appeared to be listening to them, Lillian saw that her attention was on the conversation at the adjacent table. She caught the words "Hitler," "Nazis," and "Bund," and fully expected Izzy to add her staunch support for immediate U.S. involvement.

When the voices grew louder, Lillian and Lois had no choice but to stop and listen.

"It's not our business," cried one man with a florid face. "We lost too many men in the Great War and we're not doing it again!"

"Let 'em fight it out between themselves," said another. "That's been their history. It'll burn itself out."

Lillian saw that most people supported this point of view, while others remained noncommittal, listening to all sides. A few men supported aiding England financially and with armaments, but drew the line at sending our boys over to fight. And one or two people argued for immediate involvement. She glanced at Izzy now and then, waiting for her to jump in.

Instead, Izzy was taking in the points of view of the men at the table next to theirs. She sat utterly still, except that her hand played nervously with the base of her glass, twisting it around. Lillian saw that Izzy was intently observing the copper-haired man across the way, the one they called Red. He seemed to be outnumbered in his opinions but was holding his own.

"How can you say that?" he asked. "Look what happened last year. Kristallnacht, and now the deportation of Jews. The Sudentenland, and now the whole of Czechoslovakia. Don't you see his pattern? Hitler is nothing but a liar and a thug, stringing us along with promises that he has no intention of keeping. This last year has proven that to us without a doubt. We can't stand by with our heads buried in the sand!"

"But surely this has to be sorted out by the European countries," one woman countered.

"You're clearly outnumbered, Red," said the man's friend who's chair butted against Lillian's. He leaned over to her and held out his hand. "Lloyd."

Lillian shook his hand. "Lillian Hapsey."

"So, what do you say?"

Lillian was suddenly in the spotlight and uncomfortable with voicing her opinions that shifted with the news. "I'm not sure what to believe anymore, but I do understand why people don't want to send our boys to fight someone else's war." Lois was starting to agree with her when Red spun around with a look of outrage.

"Someone else's war! Do you really believe that? Austria. Czechoslovakia. Now Poland!" With each country he slammed his hand on the table. "And they won't stop there. They've bombed ships in Great Britain, for God's sake! If we don't stop Hitler now, it will be too late." He twisted around to the man next to him who was still arguing for isolationism.

Lillian turned to Izzy, and spoke under her breath. "Goodness! He sounds just like you. Don't you think?"

Izzy remained strangely silent, yet her eyes flashed. Lillian wondered why she wasn't speaking out. Izzy was following the words of Red, twisting her glass around and around. Occasionally, Red's eyes darted to Izzy. Was it a silent challenge?

"It's not our war!" concluded the man with the florid face. "They're always fighting amongst themselves. I say leave us out of it!" He slammed down his drink and waved for another.

But Red held firm. "This *is* our war, whether we like it or not. There's no stopping him."

"But it's an ocean away," said the woman. "We shouldn't go asking for trouble."

Red spun on her now. "What makes you think he'll stop at Europe? He'll be here as soon as he can. We *must* help, now! Hitler is nothing but a bully and a – "

Izzy suddenly snapped at him. "The only bully here is you, telling everyone what to think! We're all entitled to our own opinions."

Izzy and Red glowered at each other for several fraught moments. Lillian could almost feel the crackling energy between them, and yet she couldn't read the expression on Izzy's face. The man had been saying exactly what Izzy believed. Why had she turned on him?

Red shot to his feet and left the table, followed by Lloyd, who smiled at Lillian and gave a light shrug.

Lois grabbed Sonny's hand. "Let's dance," she said. Sonny took a sip of his drink and let Lois pull him onto the floor. They were soon dancing cheek to cheek.

Lillian leaned in towards Izzy, utterly baffled. "Izzy?"

Izzy's face had softened, and she followed Red with her eyes. He went up to the bar where he joined his friends who handed him a drink and slapped him on the back, as if to humor him.

"Gotta admire a guy like that," said Izzy, her eyes still on him.

Lillian's mouth dropped open. "But – why did you chase him away?"

Izzy blinked at the floor and then turned to Lillian. "I don't know why."

"His ideas were exactly like yours – almost word for word." Lillian took a sip of her old-fashioned. "I saw the looks between you. For a moment I thought perhaps you fancied him." Lillian looked across the room, where Red was still arguing, shaking his head. "He's a handsome man, don't you think?"

Izzy's eyes never left Red. "Handsome? He's the most beautiful man I've ever seen."

Lillian didn't know what to make of it, and she was further surprised when Izzy declined a few offers to dance, something she rarely did. Izzy sipped her drink, pretending to enjoy the music, but her hand played nervously with the tablecloth or her glass, and her brow was slightly contracted.

Lillian looked across the way and saw that Red wasn't dancing either, but was in deep conversation with a few men at the bar. A serious man. Not Izzy's type at all.

Sonny and Lois sat back down and ordered drinks, Lois fanning herself with her hand. They soon had Lillian laughing with a story about an over-zealous couple on the dance floor who kept bumping into them.

Then, to Lillian's astonishment, she saw that Red was crossing the crowded dance floor, coming towards their table, followed by his friend. Surely, he wasn't coming back for more.

Red stopped in front of their table, and stood before Izzy, eyes fixed on her.

Sonny leaned in to Lois and Lillian and whispered with a laugh – "He's a brave man. You gotta give him that."

"My sis can be tough when she wants to be. Soft as pudding at heart."

Lillian found that she was holding her breath. She feared that Izzy would lash out at him again.

Instead, Izzy rose to her feet and faced Red, barely an inch away from him. Their eyes never left each other. No words were exchanged, and yet something passed between them. Their hands linked, and they moved into a dance.

Lillian's mouth dropped open, again. Just when she thought she knew Izzy …

"Care to dance?" Lloyd asked Lillian.

She accepted his arm, but her mind remained firmly stuck on Izzy's baffling behavior.

"You're surprised?" asked his friend.

"Well, yes, I have to say I am. I thought … well, I don't know what I thought."

They both glanced over at Red and Izzy. Lillian had to admit that they looked well together – both with auburn hair, tall and slim. Both with an intensity about them. When other men tried to cut in, Izzy didn't even notice. Her eyes were locked on Red – they were moving in a world of their own.

One song ended and another immediately began. When Lillian and Lloyd moved closer to the couple, Lillian had to stare. If she wasn't mistaken, Red was singing into Izzy's ear, words to the song the band was playing – "With time on my hands, and you in my arms…" Izzy nestled deeper into his arms. It looked as if they had been together for years, rather than minutes. Lillian couldn't have been more surprised.

"Looks like your friend has really gotten to Red. She's cast one helluva spell on him."

"I'd say it's the other way around," said Lillian. "I thought they disliked one another."

His friend laughed. "Look at him! He's lost all his fire. I couldn't get another word out of him. I'd say he's smitten. She married?"

"No!" Lillian said. She eyed Red. "Is he?"

"Nope."

Again, they glanced at Izzy and Red dancing, completely lost in each other. Only now they were laughing. Red was saying something to Izzy, his lips in her hair, and Izzy threw back her head and gave that full-throated laugh of hers. She pulled him closer and he twirled her around.

They were dazzling. It made Lillian happy just to watch them. She had never seen Izzy so obviously taken with a man. This was not the amused but detached Izzy she had come to know over the years. Izzy was clearly enamored.

Lloyd shook his head in disbelief. "I've never seen him like this. Does she have someone – a gentleman friend?"

"No. Does he have a girlfriend?"

Lloyd smiled wryly. "He does now."

Chapter 5

❧

On Monday the temperature dropped, and clouds darkened the day. Another day of cold rain was expected. And yet, the weekend had cheered Lillian, and she began the week in an optimistic frame of mind. As she rode the trolley to work, she ticked off the things that were going right. Most importantly, she had lined up Mrs. Crawford from the first floor to babysit for a few days. Though the elderly woman helped out in a pinch, her babysitting days were over, as she explained to Lillian. But she would be happy to help out until arrangements could be made with the Sisley sisters.

Tommy and Gabriel weren't happy about it. They complained that when Mrs. Crawford took naps, they had to be quiet. Lillian decided she would make it up to the boys by bringing Christmas into their home. She would hang their stockings from the bookshelf, and little by little fill them with small presents and candies and oranges. She would even try to get a Christmas tree this week.

Yes, she thought, smiling out at the day, she felt up to the task of Christmas.

She also had the satisfaction of completing the sewing for Mrs. Harrison. She had worked on it for several hours on Sunday, and had dropped off the parcel at the dry cleaner on her way to the trolley.

Lillian got off at her stop and walked another block, looking up at the department store. A few garlands now outlined the windows, and lights hung around the entrance. The department store was beginning the yearly transformation into a Christmas wonderland and Lillian felt a childlike surge of happiness.

Besides, she thought, with a slight shift of mood, she needed her job. After combing the want ads again on Sunday, she was more grateful than ever for her position in the dress salon, and she resolved to make herself indispensable.

"Good morning, Mr. Hinkley!" Lillian said, arriving a good fifteen minutes early.

He spun around, appearing mildly embarrassed by the friendly conversation he was having with a pretty young woman.

"Late, early, I never know what to expect from you, Mrs. Hapsey." He cleared his throat and smoothed down his pencil-thin moustache. "May I introduce you to Miss Letitia Hamm? She'll be working with us over the holidays, and possibly after," he said with a sidelong glance at Letitia.

"Welcome," said Lillian. "I'll be – "

"Nice to meet you, ma'am. I guess you'll be showing me the ropes. I have some experience, but not specifically with women's clothing, though I am a fast learner, if I may say so myself. And I have an eye for displays – 'glamorize and dramatize,'" she said, echoing one of Mr. Hinkley's most cherished maxims. She beamed up at him. "Oh, and I can pick up any shift if you need any time off."

"Mrs. Hapsey, why don't you set out the new cardigans while I show Letitia around the store."

"Gladly," said Lillian, offering a welcoming smile to Letitia.

Lillian placed her purse and sack lunch in the back room, greeted the other clerks, and began to lay out the sweaters.

She hoped that having an extra person in the department wouldn't mean fewer hours for her and the others. And yet she was relieved that Mr. Hinkley would be occupied with Letitia for much of the morning. She always felt a release of tension when he left the floor.

In between displaying the new cardigans, Lillian made several sales, chatting with her customers about their plans for the holidays.

She realized that she was actually enjoying her job, when across the way she recognized the black form of a woman. She froze. The woman was apparently looking for someone, rather than shopping. Lillian waited for her to turn in profile. Sure enough, it was Mrs. Blackham, a fellow firehouse widow who headed up the annual Christmas party committee. She should have known Mrs. Blackham would come looking for her and try to persuade her to attend the Christmas party.

Lillian inched her way to the back counter, holding a long glittering dress she had been returning to the floor, and leaned against the wall, hoping to be spared an encounter with the woman. Through the display of elegantly dressed mannequins, Lillian saw the widow glancing around in consternation. When she appeared to be crossing over to the dress salon, Lillian ducked behind the curtain that led to the store room. She stood in the back room and waited a few minutes, feeling like a coward. She slowly parted the curtain, trying to peer through the crack. Just as she was breathing a sigh of relief at not seeing the widow, the curtain was whipped back by Mr. Hinkley.

"Mrs. Hapsey! What, may I ask, are you doing? You're supposed to be on the floor!"

"I – I was just coming back out."

Mr. Hinkley looked her up and down, and narrowed his eyes in suspicion. "If I didn't know better, I would think you were hiding from some-one. The police? A creditor perhaps?"

"Indeed not!" said Lillian, flushing pink.

She went to the dress rack and hung up the evening gown, hoping the other saleswomen hadn't heard Mr. Hinkley. She felt like a common crim-inal, and threw an indignant glance at the back of his head.

Her anger shifted from Mr. Hinkley to her-self. She should have simply greeted Mrs. Black-ham, but she just wasn't up to a conversation with her. She knew the fellow widow would try to persuade her to come to the holiday party so that they could sit together, as they had the past few years.

Mr. Hinkley walked around with Letitia, explaining the layout of the department, then he stopped beside Lillian.

He rubbed his hands together. "Now! While we have a moment, I want to talk about sprucing up the department. It's time to start decorating for the holiday. Letitia – with her skills in display – will be in charge. Come, Letitia. Let's take a look and see what we have, shall we? There's a box of Christmas decorations in back."

Mrs. Olin, who had been there since the early days of Mrs. Klein, leaned in towards Lillian. "Can't say I'm surprised. He's been threatening to hire younger saleswomen."

*

The afternoon rush was busier than usual for Lillian, especially with Letitia shadowing her and asking so many questions. Still, she was a sweet girl and Lillian wanted to help her do her best.

Lillian spent the last hour of her shift unpacking and hanging several new dresses – beautiful styles for the holidays, rich in color and fabric. She looked longingly at the new dresses, imagining herself wearing them. She pulled out a crimson velvet dress with a ruched bodice – so soft and lovely. How beautifully it would go with her grandmother's ring – a pearl with clusters of glittering garnets around it. But where would she ever wear it?

She moved to a different dress – a silk day dress in cobalt blue. Perhaps she would have more use for this one. She slid the fabric between her fingers and imagined slipping on the dress and taking a sketchbook to the Metropolitan Museum. She would visit the Egyptian Art collection, and stroll through the medieval and Byzantine galleries, taking in the wealth of beauty and craftsmanship. Then she would have lunch in the tea room, and spend all afternoon sketching the European paintings and –

"Mrs. Hapsey!" Mr. Hinkley snarled in her ear. "You spend more time daydreaming than working. Sometimes I wonder what I'm paying you for."

Lillian hung up the remainder of the dresses, focusing on her task.

She left work a good half hour later than usual and found that the rain was falling heavily. Though she had planned to get a Christmas tree on her way home, by the time she caught the trolley and stopped at the bakery, there was no time for it. Six o'clock was the latest Mrs. Crawford could watch the boys, as her bedtime was at seven.

As Lillian turned onto her street, she came across Mrs. Rossi shielding her bag of groceries with an umbrella.

"Hello, Mrs. Hapsey! What do you think of all this rain?"

"Good evening." Lillian tilted her umbrella and glanced up at the sky. "I think I'd just as soon have snow."

"Soon enough," said Mrs. Rossi. "Say, did I tell you my sister got the place across the street? They'll be moving in next week."

"I knew you were hoping for that, but I hadn't heard that she got the place. Across the street from you! I'm so glad to hear it. And thank you again for having the boys over the other night. They're still talking about it." In a lower voice, she added, "They're with Mrs. Crawford for a few days, and none too happy about it."

"Can't say I blame them," Mrs. Rossi said with a laugh. "They're welcome to come over any time they like. My kids behave better when they're around."

Lillian was about to protest, but Mrs. Rossi continued.

"That's the truth! Tony idolizes Tommy, and all Mary talks about is Gabriel. I better hurry home – they'll be clamoring for dinner by now." She held the bag closer, and smiled goodbye.

Lillian continued down another block, and climbed the steps to her brownstone. She shook out her umbrella and stepped inside. Within seconds, the door to Mrs. Crawford's apartment opened and Gabriel ran out, followed by Tommy. They had obviously been waiting for her. They trudged up the stairs as Lillian spoke a few moments with the babysitter.

When Lillian reached the second floor, she heard Tommy and Gabriel bickering.

"You got to go to school. I was there all day!" said Gabriel.

"It felt like it was all day." Tommy cast a dark look at Lillian as she opened the door.

"Goodness! Was it that bad?" She ushered the boys in ahead of her. "Gabriel, what did you and Mrs. Crawford do all day?"

As Gabriel took off his shoes, he tried to recall his day. "She cleaned out her bird cage. Then she crocheted, and we listened to the radio. After that she took a nap…and we had soup." He searched his memory. "And then Tommy came, and it got better."

"You call that *better*?" asked Tommy. "I call it boring!" He plopped down on the couch.

"Me too!" Gabriel sat down next to Tommy. "But we got to listen to *Dick Tracey*. That was good."

"So, it wasn't all bad?" Lillian asked.

"I guess not," said Tommy. "I'm hungry. Can we eat?"

The boys followed her into the kitchen and sat at the table as she reheated the macaroni dish from the weekend. She sliced a few tomatoes and poured two glasses of milk for them.

"I saw Mrs. Rossi. Her sister is newly married and is moving into the building across the street from her. Isn't that nice?"

"Yeah. We met her at Dom's," said Tommy. "She's real nice. They already have their Christmas tree up. And they have an electric train that runs around it."

"With a village and a frozen lake," added Gabriel. "Hey! Lake, cake. Lake, make."

"Mr. Rossi likes trains and he's teaching Dom and Tony all about them. He let me set up the train station."

Lillian scooped out the macaroni onto their plates and set the dish in the middle of the table. "No wonder you boys love being over there so much." She always worried that Tommy and Gabriel felt the absence of their father more at Christmastime.

"And because of the food their mom makes," added Gabriel.

"The food?" asked Lillian.

"*Pizzelle* and *cannoli*," said Tommy. "She's started her Christmas baking and let us help. We chopped figs for her *cucidati* cookies. She said to tell you she'll save some for you."

"Mmm. Every year she gives me a batch because she knows how much I love them."

Gabriel took a sip of milk using both hands to lift his glass. "They always have good food and people always come over. And they play music and their mom and dad dance in the kitchen."

"Do they?" Lillian often wondered if part of the reason the boys enjoyed being with the Rossis was because it felt more like a family, with a father around.

"What about us, Mommy?" asked Gabriel. "When will we have Christmas?"

"How about we start celebrating – tonight?" asked Tommy.

Lillian dished out more macaroni for the boys, happy that they were enjoying it. "You must have read my mind, Tommy. I bought some cookies on my way home."

"Yippee!" cried Gabriel.

"Sugar cookies?" asked Tommy. "The big ones?"

"Yes. After dinner, we'll cuddle up on the couch and read a few more pages from *A Christmas Carol*. How about that?"

"But no more Jacob Marley," said Gabriel. "I don't like him."

"No. He's left the story. Next comes the part about Scrooge as a little boy."

Gabriel jerked his head back. "Scrooge was a little boy?"

"Yes, he was. And we'll read about the Fezziwigs – you'll like that part."

By the time Lillian finished reading to the boys and putting them to bed, she stepped into a hot bath, feeling somewhat hopeful. Things were moving along relatively smoothly. She could almost envision that their Christmas would be all right.

The only shadow on her happy vision was that of Mrs. Blackham. The thought of the widow had plagued Lillian all day. Her last thought before drifting off to sleep was of the widow's white hand reaching out to her.

Chapter 6

❧

Lillian had arrived to work early for several days, and had planned to get to work early again, but the morning didn't go as intended. Tommy couldn't find his homework and they spent ten minutes searching for it. He finally found it in the comic book he had been reading that was tucked beneath his pillow.

Then Lillian discovered that her shoes were still damp from yesterday's heavy rain, and after spending several minutes looking for her other pair of work shoes, she remembered that they were at the cobbler's shop.

She reached up to the box in her closet and slipped on the new pair of shoes from Annette – beautiful black pumps with cutouts on the side that gave the shoes a lacey feel. Though Lillian was saving them for special occasions, she would have to wear them today.

By the time they left the apartment, they were a good fifteen minutes behind schedule. Lillian took Gabriel's hand and hurried the boys to the

Sisley sisters. She couldn't risk falling out of their good graces. As it was, they had told her that they could only babysit through the end of the month, as they were taking on three more piano students in January and would not have the time.

She knocked on their door and leaned down to Gabriel. "Do *not* touch their piano stools. And you'll have to stay quiet while they practice their morning scales. Perhaps they'll give you cookies and milk."

"Digestive biscuits," muttered Tommy.

Though Tommy and Gabriel complained about the Sisley sisters, Lillian had a soft spot for them. They were small, delicate women, who wore their soft gray hair neatly arranged on top of their heads, in the exact same style. Lillian imagined them sitting before the same vanity mirror, their arm movements perfectly coordinated as they coiled and pinned their hair.

They were always dressed with a remarkable attention to detail. Early on, Lillian had observed that while their outfits were identical, there was always some small detail that set them apart – an ever-so-slightly different sweater clasp or belt or collar. Once, unable to locate the difference, Lillian had lingered, asking them inconsequential questions while she took a closer look. At last she discovered that Sylvia – or perhaps it was Cynthia – wore stockings with a barely discernable herringbone pattern, while the other sister's stockings were plain. Subtle.

Today, they wore dresses in a pattern of pink and green flowers with ivory crocheted collars. One of them wore a pale pink cardigan, the other pale green. No challenge there. Lillian thanked them for helping out, and hurried to catch the trolley.

She was determined that, come what may, tonight she would get a Christmas tree and surprise the boys. No more excuses. She got off at her stop and winced as she stepped down from the trolley. The stiff leather of the new shoes was already cutting into the back of her ankles. She decided that before going to the tree lot she would have to pick up her shoes from the cobbler's.

As Lillian turned the corner to the department store, she almost bumped into Letitia, who was leaning into a handsome young man and talking comfortably.

"Oh! Good morning, Mrs. Hapsey." Letitia straightened, and linked her hands behind her back.

"Good morning." Lillian nodded to them both.

Letitia bit her lip, and then broke into a smile. "This is Joe Maguire." She took his hand. "My fiancé."

"Well, congratulations! Pleased to meet you, Joe. I'm late. I'd better hurry."

"I'll be right in."

As Lillian approached the women's dress salon, she stopped on seeing the result of Letitia's decorating attempt. There was no point to anything. A crushed garland lay haphazardly on one countertop, several ornaments were scattered on the front counter, and a few small reindeer – who appeared to be lost from the herd – stared out from individual displays.

Mrs. Olin pursed her lips and lifted and dropped the end of a garland. Mr. Hinkley saw her exchange a glance with Lillian.

"You're late, Mrs. Hapsey." He cleared his throat. "Letitia didn't have much time to decorate, as we became extremely busy. Perhaps you would like to improve upon the decorations?"

"I'd be happy to," Lillian responded.

She snatched a few minutes in the morning to examine the remaining materials in the box: a few garlands, wreaths, a role of red ribbon, and ornaments. Simple would be the best approach as there wasn't much to work with. Mr. Hinkley had cleared out most of the decorations that Mrs. Klein had accumulated over the years, saying they were dusty and outdated. He made it known that he would not waste his budget on foolish holiday displays, but would instead invest in the latest mannequins from Paris.

Letitia walked up to Lillian and twisted one side of her mouth. "It didn't quite turn out like I thought it would. I can help you, if you like. If you just tell me what to do."

"Thank you, Letitia," Lillian said. She coiled the garland from the front counter and put it in the box. "Let's start fresh – see what we have to work with."

Letitia nodded and gathered the reindeer. "Mrs. Hapsey?"

"Yes?"

"You didn't say anything to Mr. Hinkley, did you? I mean, about me and Joe?"

"Of course not. I can't see that it's any business of his. Still, ..."

"What?"

"He would not like to be made a fool of."

Letitia bit her lip, and wrung her hands. "I know. I know what you mean. It's just that – I really need this job. At least until Joe gets his promotion. He works at the shipyards. He's a real good mechanic and is working his way up. As soon as he gets his promotion, we're getting married. We're saving for our wedding."

"I'm happy for you. He seems like a very nice young man."

Mrs. Olin called Letitia over. "Letitia, can you help Mrs. Graham find another size?"

Letitia gave a parting smile to Lillian and hurried over to Mrs. Olin.

In between helping women with choices for gifts, and fitting them with clothes for the holidays, Lillian decided how to decorate the dress salon. She chose a few areas that would make the greatest impression upon entering the department. As she moved about the floor, she realized how much her feet were beginning to hurt. She wished she had broken in the shoes before wearing them.

She nestled a few sparkling ornaments in a bed of cotton snow. When she raised her head, she gave a light gasp – there was Mrs. Blackham again. Lillian briefly considered speaking to her, but she had to get off her feet, if only for a moment.

Lillian was sure the widow meant well, but she just wasn't up to seeing her. For the past several years, the woman had latched onto Lillian at the annual Christmas party. The gathering itself was too much of a reminder of Tom, and of what she didn't have. And Mrs. Blackham had a way of making it worse. Every year, Lillian felt so dejected after the party that she resolved not to go again. Going to Annette's afterwards had always helped to dispel the gloom, but this year Lillian would be on her own. If she had to sit next to the widow again, she feared she would be dispirited for the entire Christmas holiday.

Though Lillian justified her reason for avoiding the widow, she still felt like an absolute coward. She stepped back out onto the floor, but Mrs. Blackham was not there. If she returned, Lillian was resolved to face her.

Between unpacking boxes, restocking the merchandise, and making sales, Lillian had placed ornaments and garlands around the department. Rather than take time to eat in the lunchroom, Lillian ate her sandwich in the back. She discreetly took off her shoes and rubbed her feet, but then they hurt even worse when she put her shoes back on. She returned to the floor, and added a few final touches to the decorations.

Mr. Hinkley noticed the difference but didn't comment – which meant that he must approve of the results. It wasn't much, but the shimmer and sparkle helped to add a holiday touch. That was that, thought Lillian, tying a final red ribbon on a display. "Now, that's an improvement!"

Lillian recognized the woman who gave the compliment as the new manager of Housewares. A friendly woman who always dressed beautifully, moved briskly, and seemed to love her job. She had a reputation for being highly effective, and Lillian had heard that the owners were impressed with her, and with the increased sales of her department.

"Thank you," said Lillian. "It adds a little holiday spirit."

"Good for sales," said the woman. "I'm Ellen Cultrain. I manage Housewares."

"Lillian Hapsey."

"Keep up the good work." And she was off.

Those few words of praise gave Lillian a tiny boost. She felt that her work had been recognized and appreciated. She looked over the department and felt that it did have a festive air to it now. Then she shook her head at herself for letting a passing remark mean so much to her.

Mr. Hinkley must have overheard the comment, for he now strode over to Lillian. "There are gift boxes to be restocked for under the counter. And make sure the pencils are sharpened and that there are enough pads."

"Yes, Mr. Hinkley."

"Quickly, now," he said, clapping his hands. "The afternoon crowd is already arriving."

The department was soon a flurry of activity, the dressing rooms were full, and Lillian had several customers to attend to. She was just returning a few dresses to the floor from the dressing rooms when her arm was tugged.

"Lilly!"

Lillian's heart leapt to see her friend.

"Izzy! What are you doing here?" Izzy never came to the store during the week.

"I decided to take the day off to do some shopping with Aunt Ethel. She's downstairs deciding between hats, so I thought I'd stop by and say hello. Besides, I just had to see you."

Lillian's eyes widened. "Red?"

Izzy nodded. "We've been out every night. I'm trying to slow it down. I keep telling myself that it's too good to be true. But it just keeps getting better and better."

"Oh, Izzy, that's wonderful!"

"We've been out to dinner and dancing – but mostly we've just talked, and taken long walks. I can talk to him about anything, Lilly, and he – "

Mr. Hinkley passed by them, recognizing Izzy as "a discerning woman of style," his favorite type of customer. He occasionally saw her shopping in the dress salon, but he hadn't quite worked out whether she was a customer of Lillian's or simply a friend.

Izzy moved to an evening gown, and lifted the fabric between her fingers. "And this one? Does it come in another color?" she asked Lillian. Izzy's disapproving side glance at Mr. Hinkley sent him scuttling back to the counter.

"I'm so happy for you, Izzy."

A fellow saleswoman, Miss Lipton, whispered into Lillian's ear. "You're wanted in the dressing room."

"I better go," said Izzy. "Aunt Ethel will be looking for me." She observed Mr. Hinkley fawning over a customer and shook her head. "You can do so much better than this."

Lillian watched Izzy hurry off. She was obviously in love. Lillian had never seen her like this.

Towards the end of her shift, there was a lull in business. Lillian was grateful for the chance to catch her breath. She organized the receipts and then began to straighten the department.

As she did so, her mind went back to Izzy and how she glowed with happiness. The way she described her time with Red reminded Lillian of her parents' relationship. They, too, had always been a romantic couple, holding hands as they took long walks together, having deep discussions, and enjoying moments with each other throughout the day.

Lillian thought of her relationship with Tom, and felt a little twinge of regret. They had not had that kind of relationship. She stared out at the floor, remembering their time together. Tom had always been wrapped up in his work, first with his job at the trolley company in Poughkeepsie. When the company closed and he lost his job, all his time was spent looking for work. He finally decided they should move to New York City. Eventually, with the help of an acquaintance, he found a position as a fireman in Brooklyn. He was always busy, and most of her time was consumed with Tommy and Gabriel. She and Tom never seemed to have time to simply enjoy each other's company, to talk about their dreams and plan for the future. And yet they had loved one another.

There were many ways of loving, she thought. Still, she was happy that Izzy had found that deeply romantic kind of love. A faint smile formed on her lips, and she let out a sigh.

"Don't just stand there!" Mr. Hinkley said. "Look busy with something!"

The department was tidy, and the only customers were already being helped by the other saleswomen. Mrs. Olin was getting ready to leave for the day, and took Lillian's arm.

"If only Mrs. Klein hadn't retired. Good night, dear."

"Good night, Mrs. Olin." Lillian had worked under Mrs. Klein for three years. Though she had been a strict manager, she had always been fair. Lillian missed her terribly.

Lillian did her usual "look busy" activity. She went to the day dresses that hung on a rack and began to unbutton a few of them, so that she could then rebutton them. She did the same with the sweaters, unfolding and then neatly refolding them.

Her feet were aching from the new shoes and she feared the blisters had broken. She glanced at the clock, counting the minutes to when she could go home, take a hot bath, and apply salve on the wounds.

Mr. Hinkley was going over the schedule at the counter with Letitia and Miss Lipton. Lillian moved to the other side of the table, and slid her aching feet out of her shoes.

She rested her feet on the cool tile and closed her eyes in relief. She would add Epsom salts to her bath tonight and –

"Mrs. Hapsey!" Mr. Hinkley hissed.

She jumped and slipped on her shoes, wincing.

"That is not allowed, as you are well aware," he said. He looked around the department and spoke in a low voice. "We are professionals here. We do not take our shoes off at work. Service and style, Mrs. Hapsey. Service and style! You may have gotten away with such behavior with Mrs. Klein, but not with me."

"It's just that these shoes are new and – "

"Please try to behave in a manner that does credit to our department."

Lillian opened her mouth to object, but changed her mind. "Yes, Mr. Hinkley."

"You took a long vacation, against my wishes, at our busiest time. You've repeatedly canceled at the last minute with excuses about babysitters. And now you're having problems with your footwear." He drew himself up and looked down his nose at Lillian. "I think perhaps you need a few days to put your affairs in order."

"No, I don't. I have everything under control, I assure you."

"Letitia!" He waved the pretty girl over. "Mrs. Hapsey requires some time off. Would you be able to work her Saturday shifts from now on?"

Lillian gasped in surprise. Surely he wouldn't do that.

"I'd be happy to help out!" she said with smile.

"That's the spirit!" He glanced disapprovingly at Lillian's shoes, and walked off.

Lillian's spirits sank at losing the days with the most commissions. Her paycheck would be significantly smaller, and she would feel it. She so wanted to make this Christmas special, but she needed money for that.

Letitia placed a hand on her arm. "Mrs. Hapsey, do you not need the days off? I thought I was helping you out." She tried to see Lillian's downturned face.

Lillian didn't trust herself to speak. She gave a little smile and continued straightening the dresses.

"I told Mr. Hinkley that I wanted as many shifts as possible, but I don't want them at someone else's expense."

"It's not your fault, Letitia. It's between me and Mr. Hinkley." Lillian pressed the girl's hand and glanced at the clock. She went in the back to retrieve her purse, thankful that the day was finally over.

For the first time since she worked at the department store, Lillian began to doubt her value as an employee. She had always believed herself to be a good worker. But perhaps it had just been Mrs. Klein's kindness that had given her that impression. Perhaps she had overestimated herself.

As she walked to the trolley, Lillian felt that she was failing, and that life was passing her by. The comments from Tommy and Gabriel stayed with her – about how much fun it was at the Rossi's house, how his parents danced together in the kitchen. Was she failing her boys as a mother? Was she doing enough? Should she attempt to find a better-paying job?

She picked up her shoes at the cobbler's, switched them immediately, and hurried to the Christmas tree lot, though she was limping in pain. The thought of a tree had buoyed her all day long, imagining how it would add pine scent and sparkle to their home. She wasn't going to change her mind now.

When she arrived at the tree lot, she tried to rouse a feeling of happiness, but failed and slumped back into fatigue.

Christmas had been such a happy time for her as a young girl. Every year she and Annette had gone with their parents to the local Christmas tree farm to pick out their tree. Then, with music playing in the background, they would decorate the tree, and enjoy the fresh-baked treats their mother made every year. And that was just the beginning of a magical Christmastime. Lillian wanted nothing more than to give her boys the same kind of Christmas – happy, secure, and full of beauty and wonder.

Lillian looked at the array of Christmas trees and tried to imagine them in her apartment. She had a moment of doubt. This would be the first time setting one up herself. She lifted a few trees. They were heavier than she expected. She would have to get a small one.

She moved from one tree to another, checking the weight. She finally chose a small tree that she could carry home on her own. But when an eager lot boy ran up and offered his assistance, she allowed him to help her. He wasn't much older than Tommy, and her heart went out to him.

They carried the tree together the few blocks, and up the stairs of her apartment building, where they propped it outside her door. The poor lad must be tired from a day of carrying trees, thought Lillian.

"Thank you for your help," she said. "I'm not sure I could have managed on my own." She reached into her purse and tipped him. "I hope you have a very Merry Christmas."

His eyes widened as he pocketed the coins. "Gee, thanks, ma'am!" He touched his cap and gave a wide smile to Lillian. Then he ran down the stairs, whistling a cheerful tune.

The neighborhood was full of boys trying to earn a little pocket money – shoveling snow, running errands, working at the newsstands. Tommy wanted to work, but she told him he was too young. And he was angry about it. As he was about so many things – having a babysitter, not being able to stay out late, or be over at Dom's all the time. Doing homework when he wanted to be playing stoop ball. Was she being too strict? She was too tired to think about it.

She brought the tree inside and took off her shoes, sighing in relief. The apartment was cold and unwelcoming. She glanced at the clock – she had half an hour to get to the Sisley sisters. First, she applied salve and band-aids to her feet. Then she took out the Christmas tree stand from the top of the closet.

It took her a while to wriggle the tree into the stand, but she finally had it secured. She took a step back, and leaned her head to one side – it looked smaller in the apartment. Perhaps she should have gotten a larger one. She set out the pan of potato soup from yesterday and checked the bread drawer. Empty. If she hurried, she could pick up some day-old bread on her way to the Sisley sisters.

She walked as quickly as she was able, first to the bakery, and then to pick up the boys.

"Mommy!" cried Gabriel, running to her.

Tommy leaned into her hug, but seemed out of spirits as they walked home. Probably just hungry and tired of babysitters. She hoped the tree would help.

When they reached their apartment, Lillian opened the door, and turned on the light. She waited for them to exclaim about the tree.

"Well?" she asked, with more enthusiasm than she felt. "What do you think?"

When the boys saw the little tree, their faces fell.

Tommy looked from the tree to her, and back to the tree, remaining silent. Instead of the burst of happiness she had hoped for, he had simply taken off his coat and shoes.

"Is that a Christmas tree?" Gabriel asked, more confused than disappointed.

Lillian assessed the tree anew. It appeared small and sad. Hopeless. "Remember, there are no lights on it yet. Or decorations. Oh, look at the time! Let me get dinner on the table. Go wash up, boys. I have a surprise for you."

She reheated the soup and put out a few additional dishes of food to make it look like a fuller dinner — a bowl of applesauce, a relish tray with carrot sticks and pickles, and several slices of bread and butter. She had one cookie left from the other day. She cut it in two and put the halves on saucers next to their glasses of milk.

As she ladled soup into their bowls, she asked them about school. But instead of talking about his time at school, Tommy complained about all their babysitters.

"Mrs. Peabody, Mrs. Crawford, the Sisley sisters. They all make us be quiet and sit up straight all the time. Before and after school isn't so bad, but I don't want to go on Saturdays anymore. It's too long."

"Me either," said Gabriel.

"Well, that's my surprise." She leaned forward and reached for their hands. "From now on, I have Saturdays off!"

Both boys stopped eating and waited to hear more.

"You mean..?"

Lillian nodded. "No babysitter on Saturday! At least for the time being."

Gabriel pushed back his chair and ran to give her a hug. "Hooray! Thanks, Mommy!"

Though Tommy rarely did anything in imitation of Gabriel, he, too, pushed back his chair and put his arms around her. He stayed there and leaned his head on her shoulder. Tommy pretended to be tough and older than his eight years, but Lillian knew that he was extremely sensitive at heart.

"What will we do?" Tommy asked, his face transformed in happiness. Lillian hadn't realized just how much it meant to him. Perhaps the other kids at school were talking about Christmas. Again, her heart ached at not providing a happy Christmas for her boys. She decided she would do whatever it took, even if she had to dip into her savings.

"I thought we could take the train into the city next Saturday to see the Christmas tree and the skaters. And we can look at all the store decorations."

"Can we take a carriage ride in Central Park?" asked Gabriel.

"And see a movie?" asked Tommy.

"Why not?" said Lillian. The happiness in their faces was priceless. She was almost grateful to Mr. Hinkley.

The rest of the evening was a happy one. Tommy even brought her the book they were reading. "I guess this is part of our celebration," he said. "We're on the Ghost of Christmas Present now."

Lillian smiled and put her arms around the boys. "If I remember correctly, he's a rather jolly fellow. You'll like him."

Gabriel ran to get his teddy bear, Taffy, and then both boys snuggled closer as she began to read.

*

After the boys were asleep, Lillian looked through the cupboard for the lights and decorations. There wasn't much, since they had always gone to Annette's for Christmas, but she would take stock and see what she needed to purchase.

As she pulled out the box with lights, she came upon her old art supplies and felt the familiar thrill they always brought. Other than her sketchbook, she had set aside any remnant of her days as an artist. She lifted the brushes and the tubes of paint, and her face softened at the memory of her old dream. She was going to be a professional painter – maybe even go to Paris one day.

Her youthful dreams had come to a halt when Tom lost his job. While he looked for work in New York City, she – pregnant with Tommy – had moved back home with her parents.

She sat in front of the little Christmas tree holding her brushes and paints. "It's too late for all that," she said softly. She returned the supplies to the cupboard and turned off the light.

Chapter 7

❦

Though Lillian smiled as Mrs. Allen, a loyal customer, described her holiday plans, Lillian's mind was on her job. She might be able to manage losing a few Saturdays, but if her work schedule were further reduced, she would have a hard time making ends meet.

"We'll have the dresses altered just as you requested, and will deliver them to you by the weekend. And if I don't see you before your trip, have a wonderful Christmas."

"Thank you, my dear. I'll see you after the holidays!"

"Goodbye, Mrs. Allen." Lillian's smile quickly dropped as she saw Mrs. Blackham talking to Letitia, pointing in her direction.

"There you are!" said Mrs. Blackham, approaching the counter with Letitia.

Lillian put her smile back on, and decided to get the confrontation over with. "Good afternoon, Mrs. Blackham. How have you – "

"I've been here several times looking for you. This nice young girl told me where I could find you, and now here you are. I don't want to disturb you while you're working, but I do want to have a word with you. Could we meet briefly after work?"

"Oh, I'm afraid I have to pick up Tommy and Gabriel early today." It was her early shift and she didn't want to miss the opportunity of spending more time with the boys.

"Tomorrow then?"

"Well, I don't get off until – "

"I can cover for you if you need to leave early," said Letitia.

"We could meet at the café across the street," suggested Mrs. Blackham.

Lillian waited a moment, unable to think of a graceful way out. "Of course. Would you prefer the tea room upstairs?"

"Heavens, no! That's too dear." She drew back at the thought.

"The café, then. I'll meet you there tomorrow at 4:30."

"I'm so glad. Tomorrow, then."

Lillian gave an inner shudder as Mrs. Blackham pressed her hand before leaving.

Mr. Hinkley had been closely observing them – the woman in black was not "a discerning woman of style." He now swept down on Lillian. "Our department is not a place for social engagements, Mrs. Hapsey."

"No," Lillian answered. "It certainly isn't."

He rushed to welcome a mother and her two daughters into the department, bowing as he greeted them. Izzy's words came to her mind: "'You can do so much better than this.'"

Letitia overheard the reprimand, and sidled up next to Lillian. "Gosh, I didn't know he was so strict about everything. Joe might stop by later – he might have some news for me. Now I wish he wasn't coming. Mr. Hinkley won't like it."

Not fifteen minutes later, when Lillian was selecting another dress for a customer in the dressing room, she saw Joe Maguire step into the department.

Letitia's face brightened and she bounced a few times on her toes. She crossed over to him, just as Mr. Hinkley stepped out from the back room. The color rose to his face at the appearance of the handsome young man smiling at Letitia.

A flash of fear crossed Letitia's face, which caused Joe to become ill at ease.

Mr. Hinkley strode over to Letitia, his chin high in the air.

Lillian felt her temper rise and she walked briskly up to Joe.

"Joe! What a nice surprise," she said, placing a hand on his arm. She turned to Mr. Hinkley. "My nephew. Shopping for a gift, Joe?"

Mr. Hinkley looked Joe up and down, suspicious of Lillian's explanation.

"Come, Letitia," Mr. Hinkley said, taking Letitia by the elbow. "Mrs. Olin could use your assistance." His eyes narrowed, and his pencil mustache twitched. Before leaving, he whispered to Lillian, "No visiting on the floor!"

Letitia walked back to the counter with Mr. Hinkley and helped Mrs. Olin wrap some merchandise she had just sold.

Joe looked from Letitia to Lillian. "Sorry, ma'am, I didn't mean to make any trouble. But I gotta talk to Letitia. I got my promotion!"

Lillian smiled at his news. "That's wonderful, Joe! Congratulations. Well deserved, I'm sure." She pointed to the opposite end of the floor. "Wait by the elevators. I'll tell Letitia to meet you there."

She went back to the dressing room and handed her customer another dress just as the woman stepped out in front of the mirror.

"Oh, dear, I really can't decide."

Lillian motioned to Mr. Hinkley. "Could you give Mrs. Morgan your opinion on these dresses? She can't decide between the rose print and the blue paisley."

Mr. Hinkley loved nothing more than to give his opinion. He soon had Mrs. Morgan convinced that the only solution to the two dresses looking so stupendously well on her was to purchase them both.

Lillian glanced behind her and saw that Letitia was slipping away.

When Mrs. Morgan agreed and happily returned to the fitting room, Mr. Hinkley dropped his fawning smile.

"Your *nephew*, Joe? This is the first I've heard about him."

"What are the names of my sons, Mr. Hinkley?" Her tone had an edge to it that he was unused to hearing.

He raised his eyebrows, and drew his head back. "Meaning?"

"If you don't know the names of my sons, why would you know the name of my nephew?"

She stepped into the dressing area where Mr. Hinkley couldn't follow, found an empty room, and dropped onto a chair. She needed a moment to regain her composure. The combination of Mrs. Blackham and Mr. Hinkley was too much.

Lillian felt only mild compunction at having lied about Joe. Letitia and Joe were clearly in love, and she couldn't bear the thought of Mr. Hinkley getting in their way – though he would add the incident to his long list of grievances against her. She cheered herself by imagining the coming Saturday, and how happy Tommy and Gabriel would be about their day in the city. She took a deep breath and returned to the floor.

As the day dragged on, Lillian caught Mr. Hinkley looking her way, as if he was plotting against her. He obviously saw through the ruse about Joe and resented it, though what was most likely upsetting him was Letitia's deception. Lillian couldn't blame him; no one liked to be made the fool.

She glanced at Mr. Hinkley, feeling a sudden rush of sympathy for him. But when he looked up, he bristled at Lillian's gaze – taking it as criticism or mockery or some other unpleasant response that he had come to expect from the world.

The afternoon drew to a close and still Letitia hadn't returned. Mr. Hinkley would be furious. Lillian saw that Miss Lipton was on the phone, an expression of concern filling her face as she wrote something down. When she gave the message to Mr. Hinkley, his face went tight, as if he was clenching his teeth. He spun on his heels and left the floor.

Lillian glanced at her watch – a half hour to go. She would straighten the day dresses. She looked forward to going home and making a nice meal for the boys. Over dinner they could discuss their plans for Saturday.

Out of the corner of her eye, she saw that Mr. Hinkley was approaching her with a quick step. Had she been staring off, daydreaming again? She noted the spark of malicious glee in his eye.

"Letitia had to leave early and I'm afraid she can't work for a few days – family issues. She's beginning to sound like you. I hope you aren't influencing her adversely. At any rate, I'm afraid it means you'll have to stay late today, and work on Saturday."

"Work on Saturday?" Lillian's heart contracted.

"That is your usual schedule."

"Yes, but you gave this Saturday to Letitia and – "

"And now she won't be in." He raised his eyebrows, daring her to refuse.

"But I – I have plans."

"Plans, Mrs. Hapsey? You'll have to change them." He caught his reflection in the mirror, and took a moment to preen – a self-satisfied smile creeping to his mouth.

Lillian felt her lip trembling. She turned away. How she despised the man. Petty, dictatorial, arrogant. She would have to call the Sisley sisters and let them know she would be late. She shut her eyes at the thought of telling Tommy and Gabriel about Saturday.

*

Lillian caught the trolley home, jostled by the crowd. The extra hours took a toll on her, and her lower back and legs ached. All she wanted was to take a bath and go to bed. However, when she stopped at the newsstand, the headlines thrust her own troubles into perspective. She overheard one customer mutter, "This might be our last happy Christmas. The whole world will soon be at war." Her heart sank at the thought.

Lillian stopped by the Sisley sisters, and apologized for being late. As she thanked and paid them, Tommy and Gabriel squeezed past her, and headed for the vestibule.

As soon as they were outside, Tommy began to grumble. "That was so boring. Why can't we stay at home alone? We don't need a babysitter. That would save you money, since you're always worried about it."

"That's enough, Tommy," she said. She was bone tired and didn't have the patience for anything else today.

"Or we could go to Dom's – "

"That's enough! I'm tired of you always complaining about everything."

Lillian so rarely rebuked the boys, that they both kept silent the rest of the way home. When they turned onto their street, they passed Mrs. Rossi.

"Hello, Mrs. Hapsey!" She leaned down to Tommy and Gabriel. "Dom and Tony have been telling me about all the things you boys are going to do on Saturday. There's no time of the year like Christmas, is there?"

Lillian inwardly groaned at her words.

"Listen," she continued. "I'm planning a small Christmas party next week. A way to welcome my sister and her husband to the neighborhood and introduce them to a few people. I'd love for you all to be there."

"Thank you," said Lillian. "My work schedule keeps changing, but I'll do my best to be there."

"You don't have to let me know now. It's an open invitation. Goodbye. You boys have fun on Saturday!"

Tommy yanked on her arm. "Can we go, Mom?"

Gabriel took her other arm. "Can we, Mommy? Will you come with us?"

"We'll see." She began to climb the steps of their stoop with her arms around the boys, but Tommy pulled away.

"We'll see?" echoed Tommy. "That means *no*! You never do anything with us."

"I'm tired, Tommy. I wouldn't be any fun. You and Gabriel can go."

"You're a *no* Mom – everything is always *no*! I feel like running away! Come on, Gabe."

He stomped up the stairs, with Gabriel running behind him, while Lillian checked the letter box.

Among the bills she saw a letter from the landlord. After staring at it for a few moments, she took off her gloves to open it. "Oh, no," she whispered, reading the notice that there would be a rent increase the following month.

She leaned against the railing to the stairs, wondering how she was going to manage. A second job? But that would leave no time with Tommy and Gabriel. More sewing. That was the only solution. Assuming she would keep her job. She didn't trust Mr. Hinkley. He had it in for her. She slowly mounted the steps.

Then she stopped. She should check with Mrs. Harrison now to pick up any sewing she might have. "Tommy! Come back here!"

"What?" He trudged back down the stairs.

"Here," she said, handing him the key. "I have to stop by Mrs. Harrison's. I'll be right back." She would have to hurry – the cleaner would close in a few minutes.

Lillian waited for Mrs. Harrison to finish up with her customers before asking if there was any sewing to be done. There were only two blouses that needed mending and a skirt that required a hem. Lillian thanked her and promised to have them finished in a day.

Disappointed that there wasn't more, Lillian considered going to other dry cleaners to see if they needed any tailoring done. It would be a waste of time, she thought. They all did their own sewing, as Mrs. Harrison had before her arthritis became too bad.

Lillian wished she hadn't taken her frustration out on Tommy. She had overreacted to his words about not wanting a babysitter.

Her head snapped up as she remembered his words. Surely, he wouldn't really run away, would he? She picked up her pace. Then she began to run. What if the boys were gone when she got home? What if she couldn't find them? She rounded the corner onto her block, and rushed to their stoop. In her hurry, she caught her foot on the step, stumbled and fell. She rose quickly, opened the door, and ran up the stairs.

She mounted the top step, her heart pounding. Her hand shook as she flung open the door.

"Tommy!"

"What?" he asked, annoyed.

"What happened, Mommy?" asked Gabriel, his teddy bear in hand.

Lillian stood in the doorway, flooded with relief. She was ready to burst into tears, but she tried to appear composed. She took off her hat and coat.

"Blood!" cried Gabriel, pointing at her leg. He ran up to her.

She looked down and saw that her knee was bleeding. "It's nothing. I tripped on the step is all. Tommy, can you set the table while I change? I'll be right out." She limped down the hall to her bedroom.

Tommy groaned and went into the kitchen.

Gabriel followed him. "We'll help you."

"We?" scoffed Tommy.

"Me and Taffy."

"Gabriel. Taffy's a stuffed animal. You know he's not real, right?"

"I know that, but *he* doesn't."

Tommy groaned again. "Just stay out of my way. If anything breaks, I'll really be in trouble."

Lillian carefully took off her stockings and inspected them. They were ruined. She slipped on a housedress and went to the bathroom to wash her wounds and apply ointment. She wanted to lie down, turn off the light, and fall into a deep sleep. But the boys needed to be fed. And she had to tell them about Saturday – they would be so disappointed. Once again, she thought how relieved she would be when Christmas was behind her.

*

Over dinner, Tommy was largely silent, but Gabriel babbled on about how much fun the Rossi's party would be. "Their aunt is nice. Last time she colored with us and showed us how to draw Mickey Mouse and Donald Duck. Even Mary can make a duck."

"It will be nice to have her for a neighbor, won't it?"

"Yeah," said Tommy, finally speaking up. "She asked us what we were doing for Christmas. I told her we're going to see the tree at Rockefeller Center on Saturday and do some other Christmas things."

Lillian had to look away. "I'm afraid we'll have to find another day for our outing. I have to work now on Saturday."

Tommy's head whipped up and his eyes filled with anger. "I knew you'd do that! Now I have to tell all my friends we're *not* going!"

"Don't overreact Tommy, it's just a postponement. We'll see the tree. I promise."

"Yeah, just like we saw the World's Fair." He scrunched up his mouth and smashed his peas with his fork

They ate in silence. After a few minutes Gabriel looked up. "If we run away, Tommy, where would we go?"

"Don't be a dope, Gabe."

Lillian looked at him sternly, but Tommy ignored her and stabbed at his salad.

"Can Mommy come with us?"

Tommy set his fork down with a bang. "Will you shut up about it? We're not going anywhere, and we're not having Christmas, so you can just forget about it!"

"Tommy!" Lillian said firmly.

"What? How come we're the only ones without Christmas, without any fun, without a dad?" His mouth trembled at the last word.

Lillian sat stunned for a moment. She stood abruptly and began to clear the table. In order not to collapse into despair, she resorted to anger. "What's wrong with you? Can't you see I'm trying my best? You aren't making things better with your complaining and rude manners. Why don't you try to help out for a change?"

Both boys blinked at her outburst. She put the dishes in the sink and cleared the rest of the table. "Go take your bath! Go on, both of you."

Lillian washed the dishes, cleaned up the kitchen, and then went into the living room. She sat on the couch and inspected her knee. She had put salve and a band-aid on it but it still hurt, and there would be an ugly bruise. From the bathroom she heard the water filling the tub and Tommy and Gabriel arguing over Taffy.

"No teddy bears!" cried Tommy.

"But he doesn't want to be alone."

Lillian took out her sewing basket and stared at the spools of threads and needles and scissors. She had no heart for her task.

Instead, she lifted her sketchbook from underneath the couch and opened it on her lap. She took the pencil from inside the book and drew a few lines. The sketchbook was a small refuge, somewhere she could always turn, her silent communication with the world.

But no image came to mind. She looked at the page and saw it as a representation of her life – largely blank, uninspired, random efforts that added up to very little. She closed the sketchbook and placed it back beneath the couch.

What a dismal Christmas. Tommy angry. Her rent raised. Mr. Hinkley spiteful. And the meeting with Mrs. Blackham tomorrow! She groaned at the mere thought, and considered canceling.

No, she decided. She would spend a few minutes with the woman over coffee and stand firm about not attending the firemen's party.

Lillian heard the boys splashing in the bath – making explosion sounds. The floor would be wet. She sat up and was about to tell them to stop. Instead, she slumped back down and decided to let them play.

She picked up one of the blouses and inspected the hem. She threaded a needle and made a few fine stitches, remembering the past years at the firemen's Christmas party. For months after Tom's death, she had avoided the gatherings. The expressions and words of pity always set her crying. But his friends from the firehouse had pressed her about the party and she didn't have the heart to refuse them. It would be good for the boys, she'd thought.

She wasn't the only widow there, of course, though most of them had remarried after a few years – no one wanted to be alone, after all. But she had no heart for that path. Yes, the memory of Tom was softening. The raw pain was gone. But that part of her life was closed, the door locked, the key long ago tossed away.

She remembered that first party on her own. How she had dressed up, and enjoyed seeing Tommy and Gabriel playing with the other kids. Then Mrs. Blackham had latched onto her and hadn't let go. Every year was a repeat of that first year.

Though it was an ungenerous thought, Lillian had the impression that Mrs. Blackham enjoyed her widowhood. She still wore black and declared that she always would. She tried to give Lillian pointers on dealing with her loss, but the result was that Lillian left the party feeling even more alone, more bereft. It took months to shake off the effect.

Some of the other wives gossiped that Mr. Blackham had been a hen-pecked husband and that his wife's love for him arrived only after he had departed. Lillian had largely discounted the talk, assuming it couldn't be true.

She gave a slight shudder, remembering the first time she met Mrs. Blackham. The partygoers had just sung a few Christmas songs, accompanied by a piano, which Lillian enjoyed. She smiled as she watched Tommy and Gabriel eating Christmas treats at the children's table. A few green-clad elves presided over the group until the big moment when Santa himself would arrive.

Her focus was on the boys when she felt a tug on her arm. A white hand clutched her wrist. Lillian looked up and saw a woman in black taking the seat next to her. Whenever Lillian remembered that moment, her mind transformed the hand into a white skeletal claw, and she felt an irrational sense of dread.

The woman, Mrs. Blackham, had introduced herself, and was soon slathering Lillian in pity. She told Lillian about how she lost her husband eight years ago, and all the details about getting the news, the shock, the despair, the loneliness, the darkness that filled her life. Lillian had felt that she was drowning.

"It comes as a shock," Mrs. Blackham had said, again placing her hand on Lillian's arm. "And it really doesn't get any easier. I know how you feel." She tightened her clutch on Lillian's wrist. "Suddenly, your life is over. Your life is over." She shook her head sadly.

Those words had hit Lillian hard. The final nails in her coffin, shutting her in. She had swallowed those words, recognizing them as her own feelings. Every single year Mrs. Blackham sought out Lillian. Though the widow's words might be slightly different, the message was always the same: your life is over.

Lillian looked up from her sewing. It had been four years since Tom's death, and life had stopped.

Sometimes she heard Tom's voice reprimanding her: "Don't use me as an excuse. Get on with your life."

She had grieved and relived their years together over and over. It was time to move on. She knew that. Time to embrace life. That's what Tom would have wanted. He had often chastised her for getting stuck on an idea, an emotion. She could almost hear him, echoing the words of Annette and Izzy: "Come on, it's time to live! Life is short enough as it is."

And yet she remained stuck like a stream that was blocked. She thought of the creek in the meadow where she and Annette used to play as girls, gathering sticks and branches of leaves to dam up the flow. One day she'd found the water had turned all muddy and stagnant. She had felt pity for the stream and had broken the dam. As the fresh water rushed through – gurgling and sparkling in the sunlight – her heart had flooded with happiness.

She had the same urge now to clear out the debris that was causing her to stagnate – the oppressive dread of Mrs. Blackham, the petty conniving of Mr. Hinkley, the terrible news filling the newspapers, and her own crippling fears.

Stuck, she thought. I'm stuck and I don't know how to get unstuck. She looked at their pathetic little Christmas tree. She wanted the holiday to be over. This time of year only made everything worse.

She set the blouse aside. A jumble of words ran through her mind: Gabriel's, "Is that a Christmas tree?" The widow's pronouncement, "Your life is over." Tommy's words, "You're a *no!* Mom," and tonight, "How come we're the only one without a dad?"

She looked over at Tom's smiling photo next to the armchair, and she inwardly cried out to him: *Oh, Tom, I need you! I can't do this on my own.* She choked back her tears, and dropped her head in her hands. Then the tears brimmed and fell down her cheeks.

Tommy was just about to step into the living room, when he saw her hang her head and weep. He quickly stepped back into the hall, ducked into his room, and began to crack his knuckles.

When Gabriel came out of the bathroom, Tommy waved him over, and closed the door behind him.

"What?" asked Gabriel.

"I made Mommy cry."

"That wasn't very nice." Gabriel started to open the door, but Tommy kept his hand on it.

"We have to do something about it, Gabe. We – we have to make her happy."

"Okay. How?"

Tommy blinked and thought, but was unable to come up with a solution.

"I could draw her a picture," Gabriel suggested.

Tommy screwed up his mouth in skepticism.

"We could both draw her a picture."

"Nah."

"How about we clean our room?"

Tommy shook his head and cracked his knuckles again. "What makes her happy?"

Gabriel picked up Taffy and sat on the bed, giving it some thought. "She likes holding Abigail. And singing her to sleep."

"Abigail's not here, Gabriel! Think! What else?"

Gabriel looked up at the ceiling, and brightened. "Cupcakes! Aunt Annette's toffee?"

Tommy shook his head at each suggestion, and then plopped down on the bed.

"Mommy says we're her happiness," said Gabriel. "You and me."

Tommy sat up, hopeful. "You're right. She always says if we're happy, then she's happy. Good thinking, Gabe. So, here's the plan. We have to pretend to be really happy. Extra happy. Think you can do it?"

"Sure!"

Before Tommy could coach him a bit, Gabriel ran out with Taffy and jumped on the couch. "Hi, Mommy!" he said, with a big smile.

Lillian averted her face and wiped the tears from her cheeks. "All done with your bath?" She lifted his hand and kissed his wrinkled fingers. "I let you stay in the water for too long."

"No, you didn't," said Tommy, standing in front of her. "We had fun!" He also gave a big smile.

Gabriel bobbed his head up and down.

Lillian glanced at Tommy and then Gabriel. "Well, good." She resumed her sewing. "Are you boys going to listen to your show?"

Tommy ran to the bookshelf. "How about we read some more of our book?"

"Dickens?" Lillian set aside her sewing. "All right. I wasn't sure whether you boys were really enjoying the story."

"We LOVE it!" cried Gabriel.

Tommy poked Gabriel, and handed the book to Lillian.

"Well, I'm glad to hear it. Let's see...where were we?"

Tommy and Gabriel nestled on either side of her, exchanged glances and nodded. When she turned to them, they put on their happy smiles.

Her brow creased in perplexity, and she opened the book. She had left off with the Ghost of Christmas Present, and the two starving children huddled under his robe – Ignorance and Poverty. That detail had haunted her. She turned to Stave Four: "The Last of the Spirits."

Lillian read about the dark-cloaked spirit who moved like a mist upon the ground and showed no face or body except for its pointing white hand. She worried that Gabriel would be afraid, and kept glancing down at him. But each time he gave her a smile brimming with joy.

She remained puzzled, but continued reading.

However, when Scrooge himself became scared, and then grew so terrified that he could barely stand, Gabriel shot a troubled glance to Tommy.

Tommy gave a quick shake of his head, in warning.

Gabriel burst out into false laughter. "I like this ghost!"

Lillian looked down at him, surprised. "I think this spirit is supposed to be scary." She continued reading, describing the shadowy, silent ghost. But when Gabriel gave another belly laugh, Tommy burst out in anger.

"You always overdo it!"

"No, I don't!"

"Yes, you do!"

"No, I – "

Lillian lowered the book. "Overdo what? What's going on?"

Tommy looked away.

"Tommy?"

He crossed his arms and remained silent.

She turned to Gabriel and raised her eyebrows. "Gabriel?"

"Tommy said you're sad. We wanted to make you happy."

Lillian closed the book and set it on her lap. "So that's it."

"Sorry, Mommy," said Tommy. "I didn't mean to make you sad." His voiced quivered and tears filled his eyes.

She wrapped her arms around him and kissed him. "Tommy, that's not it. You didn't do anything to sadden me. I'm just…I'm just tired. That's all."

"But I'm making it worse," he said, crying freely. "I'm not helping."

Gabriel was now crying too.

"No, no, no!" she said, smiling. "Sometimes mommies just get tired and cranky. That's all." She wrapped her arms around their shoulders and squeezed them. "My boys! You two are my happiness. Nothing in this whole wide world makes me happier than you."

They looked up, hopeful.

She kissed them and smiled. "I'm happy now, you see? And we're all going to be happy from now

on. And we're going to have a happy Christmas."
She tilted Tommy's chin up. "Do you believe me?"

He nodded, and sniffled.

"And you, too?" she asked Gabriel.

"Yes," he said, lifting his pajama top to wipe
his face.

"Come," she said, standing. "It's getting late.
Let me tuck you in. We'll all have sweet dreams,
and then we'll start all over tomorrow." She put her
arms around them and walked them to their room.

Gabriel climbed into bed. "Will you tell us a
story?"

"All right." She tucked them in, kissed their
foreheads, and turned off the light. Then she sat on
the edge of their bed and began one of the stories
she often told them, about two little boys who lived
in a magical forest.

Within minutes they were asleep. Lillian told
herself that she would have to be more careful, that
the boys felt every nuance of her worry and fear.
Poor, sweet boys, blaming themselves.

She went to bed, ready to sink into sleep. And
yet she couldn't shake the sadness and fear inside
her. She lay on one side, then on the other, restless
and worried. Her mind filled with the Ghost of
Christmas Present and the two frightened children
under his robes – when they lifted their heads, she
saw the haunted faces of Tommy and Gabriel, and
her heart clenched anew.

She was afraid. Afraid of failing her boys.
Afraid of the future. Afraid of not having enough
money. She saw the bony finger of the Ghost of

Christmas Yet to Come, pointing to a bleak future. Then it changed into Mrs. Blackham's white hand clutching Lillian's wrist, as the widow repeated the words, "Your life is over."

Lillian rolled on her side and tried to keep her mind focused on the next few weeks. Where would she ever get the strength to carry on and face everything? Problem. Solution. Problem…

Christmastime 1939

Chapter 8

⌒⌒

Christmas was arriving, whether or not Lillian was ready. As she made her way to the trolley the following morning, she noticed Christmas wreaths on the neighborhood doors, and in the windows hung the artwork of children – paper angels, stars, and snowflakes. Closer to work, the awnings over the shops and storefront windows were trimmed with garlands and lights. It was impossible not to feel the approach of Christmas.

When she entered the dress salon, Mr. Hinkley waved her over. "Before you begin, I want you to sort these tickets. Letitia left them in a mess. Apparently, she won't be coming back."

"At all?" Lillian asked, surprised.

Mr. Hinkley fixed her with a glare. "Thanks to your influence. I believe you encouraged her to be insubordinate."

"I did no such thing. I – "

"She saw you visiting with all sorts of people, and thought she could do the same."

Lillian opened her mouth to defend herself, but he cut her off. "Not now, Mrs. Hapsey. There are customers on the floor." He gave a pert nod towards the lone customer looking at dresses. "Go see to them."

He had a way of keeping her down and dispirited. Lillian couldn't imagine years, or even months, working for such a person. He battered her all morning with a series of commands: "Unpack these boxes," "Ring up this garment," "Help Mrs. Olin with the mannequin," "Cover Miss Lipton's break," "Restock the counter."

When lunchtime came, Lillian went to the lunchroom feeling utterly dejected. She didn't want to work for Mr. Hinkley anymore. She was exhausted by his constant commands and worn down by his petty jabs. And she didn't want to meet with Mrs. Blackham. The encounter was sure to make her feel worse.

Lillian dropped onto a chair, and stared at her sack lunch. She wasn't hungry. Christmas music played in the background, making her even more aware of her dismal state of mind.

She had made a mess of her life. No direction, bumping along from obstacle to obstacle. She stared ahead, trying to understand the quagmire around her, and wondering how she would break free. She felt that some key part of her life was missing – that her dreams had flown far away without her.

No point in going down that path, she thought. She took out her sketchbook and pencil and began to draw a different world.

Absent-mindedly, she tapped the pencil on the paper a few times, as if getting an ink pen to flow, or coaxing tiny sparks from dry kindling. She drew a few tentative lines. With the boys and Christmas on her mind, a shape began to emerge – a wreath in a window, with a bow and snowflakes falling in front of it.

She tilted her head at the image, and then drew a window around it, and a brownstone apartment building. She drew in a stoop, and snow piled up on the sidewalk. On the page opposite, she began to draw an interior scene – a Christmas tree in a lovely apartment. It was far larger and cozier than hers. She drew a fire blazing in the fireplace and a mirror above the mantel. A smile softened her face. The tension in her shoulders eased. Her smile widened as she sketched two stockings filled to the brim, hanging from the mantel. Arranged above them, a few of her favorite Victorian Christmas postcards –

"Well!" came a voice over her shoulder.

Lillian jumped and quickly covered the drawing with her hand.

"I'm sorry, I didn't mean to startle you," said Mrs. Cultrain from Housewares. She gazed down at the cozy scenes. "Why, Mrs. Hapsey, you're an artist!"

"Oh, well, not really. I just dabble now and then."

"That's more than just dabbling." She placed her hand on the back of the chair next to Lillian. "May I join you?"

"Of course."

She took a seat next to Lillian and set her lunch down. "I only have a few minutes, but it does feel good to get off my feet."

Lillian smiled, and opened her sack lunch. "I know what you mean." They began to eat their sandwiches and talk about the department store and the coming holiday.

"I hope I'm not being intrusive," said Mrs. Cultrain, "but would you mind showing me some of your drawings?"

"There's nothing much to show, but you're welcome to take a look." She handed her sketchbook to Mrs. Cultrain. A faint blush rose to Lillian's cheeks. Outside of classes and her family, she had never shown her drawings to anyone.

Mrs. Cultrain leaned in closer to the sketches of gray skies and office buildings, of trolley cars and bustling streets. She laughed outright at the two mischievous boys with their hands in a cookie jar, and cooed at the same two boys in bed asleep with a teddy bear between them. She looked up at Lillian and regarded her anew.

"These are absolutely marvelous! You've obviously studied. Quite a lot, I should think."

"Mostly self-taught," Lillian said with a laugh. "I had an excellent teacher in high school who really encouraged me. And then I studied a year at a small art school. Tom, my husband, worked in Poughkeepsie at the time. After we married and moved there, I enrolled in the school. And loved every minute of it."

"Sounds wonderful." Mrs. Cultrain continued paging through the sketchbook.

A spark of excitement animated Lillian as she remembered that hopeful time in her life. "We had the top floor of a pretty little place, and I had an alcove all my own where I used to work. I could see the Hudson River from the window. I made countless drawings of that view."

Mrs. Cultrain looked up. "What happened? Why did you study only a year?"

Lillian came back to the present, and her shoulders slightly slumped. "Tom lost his job. He had a good position with the trolley company there, but they started to cut back. There were so few jobs back then." Lillian shook away the memories. "So, Tom came to the city to look for work and I moved back home with my parents in Rhinebeck. Eventually, Tom found work as a fireman and I joined him in Brooklyn. Along with our new-born. A few years later I had our second child."

"I think I know the rest. It sounds like my own path," Mrs. Cultrain said. "But I'm finally getting back on track. Three children later. How about you? Do you still study?"

Lillian shook her head. "Tom died four years ago. Since then, I've just focused on raising my boys and holding things together."

She appreciated that Mrs. Cultrain didn't gasp and offer her pity or say how terrible it must be for her. Instead, she gave Lillian a small nod of deep understanding.

"Perhaps someday I'll pursue it again." Lillian was surprised to hear herself admit it. It was as if the conversation had encouraged the old dream to show its face again.

"And so you should. A talent like yours shouldn't be buried away. It must be embraced, nourished, and cultivated."

The two women sat quietly for a few moments, eating their lunches, and lost in thought. Then Mrs. Cultrain brushed the crumbs from her fingers, and waved her arm, as if clearing away the cobwebs of the past. She crossed her arms on the table and leaned in closer.

"Listen. You know I'm relatively new here, but I want to do my best to take Housewares in another direction. 'Christmas Night,' the store's big shopping event, is just around the corner and I want to try something different for my department. Nothing elaborate. I think you might be able to help. Would you be interested?"

"I'd love to help – but how?"

"I have an idea for some creative merchandising, using illustrations scattered throughout the department." She used her hands to help describe the vision. "What I have in mind are cozy images of home – a fire in the hearth, a mother baking cookies with her little girls, a father reading to his sons." She gestured to Lillian's sketchbook. "Wreaths, stockings hanging from the mantel, a Christmas tree, happy children."

Lillian nodded as she envisioned the ideas.

"And here's the hook," said Mrs. Cultrain. "Added to the drawings, will be a few well-chosen items from Housewares – a canister set, shiny new pots and pans, holiday dishtowels, a table set with Fiesta dinnerware."

Lillian smiled at the images. "I like the idea. The comforts of home for the holidays – family, traditions – and shopping."

Mrs. Cultrain gave a firm nod. "Exactly!"

"And you would want me to…?"

"Design and execute the drawings." Her excitement dropped when Lillian remained silent. "Oh, but perhaps this wouldn't interest you. Or you wouldn't have the time?"

"No, no, I would love to make the drawings. It's exactly the kind of thing I always wanted to do. I'm just surprised."

"I would pay you, of course."

Lillian sat back in her chair and pressed her hand to her chest. "It would be my pleasure to make the drawings. But I can't take any money from you."

Mrs. Cultrain threw up her hands. "Then I can't accept. This is business, and I've got a budget. I'm competitive, Mrs. Hapsey. I want to win best department this year. Are you in?"

This was precisely what Lillian used to dream about – being an illustrator. "I'm in. Yes. I'd love to!" This was the closest Lillian had ever come to making a deal. She felt both awkward and euphoric.

Mrs. Cultrain shook Lillian's hand. "Deal!"

Lillian squeezed her hand and laughed. "I can hardly wait to get started." She noticed the clock and saw that she was five minutes late.

Mrs. Cultrain followed her glance. "Let's talk on our way back." They hurriedly cleared away their lunches and headed out of the lunchroom.

While they walked Lillian made notes in her sketchbook as Mrs. Cultrain described the key scenes she wanted. "I'd love to have about four or five paintings in vibrant colors with the signs of Christmas in each of them. Let's start with some rough drafts and we'll work out the details. In the meantime, I'll choose the items I'd like to feature."

"How soon do you need the sketches?"

"A few days, if possible."

"Of course! I'll have several for you to choose from." Lillian stopped just outside her department. There was Mr. Hinkley. He gave a curt nod to Mrs. Cultrain, glanced at Lillian, and down at his watch. Then, spotting one of his customers entering the department, he hurried to gush a greeting.

Mrs. Cultrain smiled at Lillian. "I'm so glad we spoke, and I look forward to working with you."

"Thank you, Mrs. Cultrain." Lillian was about to hurry away, when Mrs. Cultrain tugged Lillian's sleeve and leaned in towards her.

"Don't let that man bully you."

Lillian smiled at the advice and parted from Mrs. Cultrain.

The afternoon flew by. Lillian was filled with new-found energy. It seemed she was making more sales and enjoying herself more. Mr. Hinkley kept a close eye on her and barked a few orders, but they rolled right off her and she greeted them all with a smile.

In the middle of hanging a few dresses, she stopped – what had happened? Why did she feel so different? She stared down at the floor, and a smile slowly suffused her face – she had placed her hand on her touchstone. Her old dreams of being an artist had sprung to life! They hovered before her in sharp details, welcoming and enticing, there for the asking.

In a flash, she knew what she was going to do. She stood amazed at her audacity, but she knew it was the right thing to do. She was going to call off work tomorrow and give the whole day to her dreams. She would work on the drawings and, if Izzy was still available, she would meet her for lunch. She would see the inside of Rockwell Publishing and get an idea of how other women worked in an office environment. Just the thought of being among all those tall buildings full of possible jobs made everything seem suddenly attainable.

Mr. Hinkley cleared his throat, as he positioned himself next to Lillian. "Mrs. Hapsey, I've reworked the schedule and I'm afraid you're going to have to work the next three Saturdays."

"And I'm afraid I have to decline, Mr. Hinkley," Lillian responded pleasantly. "I have plans that I can't change."

His eye and mouth twitched, but he held her gaze. "You misunderstand me. I'm not asking you. I'm telling you."

Lillian smiled again. "And I'm refusing." She began to hang up the dresses.

"Mrs. Hapsey!" He narrowed his eyes, and drew himself up. "I would hate to see you lose your position over your refusal."

"Do what you have to do, Mr. Hinkley. Oh, and by the way, I won't be in tomorrow. I'll of course make sure my shift is covered."

He stood with his mouth open for several seconds, then spun around and stormed off the floor.

Mrs. Olin returned a dress to the same rack, and beamed at Lillian. "I wish Mrs. Klein could have witnessed that."

Lillian laughed at the remark. "I have to make a phone call. I'll be right back."

On her way to the phone booths, Lillian wondered why she hadn't stood up to Mr. Hinkley sooner. The conversation she had with Mrs. Cultrain had strengthened her, made her brave. For the first time in a long time, she felt valued.

She waited for a phone booth to be free, then she stepped inside, and placed her call to Izzy.

*

Izzy was elated to hear that Lillian was finally coming into the city to meet her for lunch and see Rockwell Publishing. Consequently, the dread of meeting with Mrs. Blackham had been greatly diminished.

After work, Lillian stepped into the café and found Mrs. Blackham at a table near the window. She took a deep breath and walked over to greet her.

"There you are," Mrs. Blackham said to Lillian, with a weak smile. "I came early and ordered a cup of coffee." A wave of concern clouded her face. "How are you? You look tired, you poor thing."

"I'm fine. I'm actually very well, thank you." Lillian took her seat. She knew she was supposed to reciprocate and ask how the widow was, but she didn't. She wanted to steer the conversation away from the predictable gloom.

"Have you been doing your Christmas shopping?" Lillian asked brightly, pulling off her gloves.

"No. I went to Gerald's grave this morning. I do miss him." She placed her hand on Lillian's wrist and Lillian flinched internally. "It's hard for us to be left all alone, isn't it? Especially at this time of year."

"Yes. Yes, it is." Lillian ordered a cup of tea and scanned the menu. "Are you going to order anything? A pastry perhaps? Or a sandwich?"

"No, no. I don't have much of an appetite." She gave a far-off look and sighed. "The years don't change that, do they?"

Lillian glanced at the menu, steeled herself, and smiled at the waiter. "I'll have a piece of chocolate cake."

Mrs. Blackham's eyebrows shot up. "I'm glad to see that one of us has an appetite."

Lillian ignored the words that were meant to hook her – the widow's words were all barbed, meant to snare and pull her down. Resentment, fear, and pity mixed in Lillian, and she began to question her decision to meet with the woman.

A waitress came and offered to add hot coffee to Mrs. Blackham's cup. The widow made a show of covering her cup, shook her head, and gave a limp smile.

"I set up our Christmas tree," ventured Lillian. "Just a small tree. I put the lights on but we still have to decorate it. I think over the weekend we'll – "

"With Gerald gone, I find it difficult to get in the holiday spirit."

"But surely after so many years you've managed to find a way?" Lillian's tea was set in front of her. She stirred in two spoons of sugar and poured in some cream. "I'm sure that's what your husband would have wanted for you."

Mrs. Blackham stiffened. "I keep his memory in the manner that best suits me, thank you." She took a sip of her coffee.

A pang of guilt shot through Lillian. "Of course, you do. You're a credit to his memory." Lillian sipped on her tea. When her cake was set in front of her, she suddenly had no appetite for it.

Mrs. Blackham took the lace hankie that was tucked inside her sleeve and dabbed her eyes.

"Wouldn't you like a fresh cup of coffee, Mrs. Blackham? Something hot on this cold, wintry day?"

Mrs. Blackham raised her eyes, but didn't speak. And yet Lillian heard the unspoken words: *A cup of hot coffee would be futile against the strength of my grief.*

Lillian sat up straight and took another sip of tea. "They say we might have snow tomorrow. Wouldn't that be nice? Perhaps we'll have a white Christmas!"

Mrs. Blackham's mouth turned up slightly, but her eyes remained damp. "Mrs. Hapsey, I think you know the reason I wanted to meet with you. It's about the annual firemen's Christmas gathering. I understand that you declined our invitation."

"The invitation from the firemen? Yes, I did. We won't be going this year."

"Mrs. Hapsey, I understand how hard it is to go on. No one knows this better than I." She placed her white hand on Lillian's wrist. "But we must face our loneliness. Even though it doesn't get any better. Our loss is permanent, after all." Her grip tightened in what Lillian supposed was meant as reassurance, but felt like entrapment. All Lillian's recent euphoria vanished as the hand tugged her back into misery.

Lillian withdrew her arm, and picked up her fork. She cut into the cake, and stared at it, almost giving in to the darkness.

But today a stubborn voice inside her said *No! Not this time. You are not dragging me down with you!* Perhaps her strength came from the call with Izzy, or from her plans with Mrs. Cultrain, or perhaps she was just tired of feeling low. Lillian's intention was to be pleasant, but a bubble of anger began to rise.

Again the white hand clasped Lillian's wrist. "Our lives may be over, but we must carry on as best we can."

Lillian jerked her arm away. "Mrs. Blackham, I'm afraid you misunderstand me. I – I don't feel as you do. Of course, I miss Tom, and yes, Christmas is difficult without him here, especially for Tommy and Gabriel. But I *am* going to be happy. I am *not* going to wear my loss like a dark cloak over me, shutting out the world. Tom would have hated that! I'm going to be strong for him and for my boys, and I'm going to be happy! Yes, happy! Your dark words pull me down every time I see you, and I don't want to hear them anymore."

Mrs. Blackham, aghast, clutched her hankie, and her hand flew to her chest. "As a fellow widow, I'm merely trying to console you."

"No, you're trying to pull me down with you." More clearly than ever, Lillian realized that Mrs. Blackham enjoyed her widowhood. It gave her status, pity, and an identity to shape to her life – the poor grieving widow. Lillian's lips rose in revulsion.

Mrs. Blackham took out a coin and placed it on the table. She slowly pulled on her gloves.

Lillian knew she was waiting for an apology, but she wasn't going to get one. Lillian ate a bite of cake, chewing with determination.

"You've made yourself perfectly clear, Mrs. Hapsey. I'm glad to know where you stand. Good day." She slid her purse over her arm, brushed at her coat, adjusted her hat, and tugged at her gloves.

But rather than offer an apology, Lillian took another, rather large bite of cake. Mrs. Blackham lifted her chin ever so slightly and left the restaurant.

Lillian was about to take another bite of cake, but set her fork down. She hadn't meant to speak in such a manner. She certainly didn't want to make

Mrs. Blackham feel bad. She jumped to her feet, and caught the widow just outside the cafe.

The widow's eyes revealed a hint of triumph. "Yes?"

"Mrs. Blackham, I hope you will be happy one day. Life is too short, too precious, to live it in any other way." She impulsively embraced the widow.

Mrs. Blackham took a step back, stunned by the audacious suggestion. "Happy?" She blinked, and looked around her, as if seeing a different future. A door seemed to open, and vulnerability flooded her face. For a brief moment, Lillian saw the young woman Mrs. Blackham used to be. Then the flash of hope turned to fear, and the door was shut with a slam. She gave a huff and quickly walked away.

Lillian went back inside, and sat down at the table. She realized that she had finally broken free of the widow's gloom. For the first time, Lillian understood that she had been focusing on Tom's death, not his life – not the happy years, his time with the boys, not the wonderful man he had been.

Lillian replayed the past few years in her mind and questioned why she had so readily embraced such a dark view of life. Perhaps it had seemed true at the time. Her life had felt over. Her life had been so entwined with Tom's, that she had become lost in him. His choices had become her choices, his decisions had become hers, his life had become hers.

But now it was time to live her life, to reclaim her old self, and pursue her old dreams. It was time to become the person she always wanted to be.

She finished the cake, only now fully tasting and enjoying the creamy chocolate. She paid her bill, and stood tall and straight as she slipped on her gloves.

As she walked down the sidewalk to catch the trolley, she felt that her very stride was different – brisk and sure. She held her head high. Her mind fluttered with all the things she was going to do with her life, for all the happiness that life had to offer — there for the asking.

Chapter 9

Lillian awoke early, excited about her day in the city and lunch with Izzy. She decided to surprise the boys with their favorite breakfast, and by the time she roused them, there was a plate of hot pancakes on the table.

"Pancakes!" cried Gabriel.

"Is it a special day?" asked Tommy.

"Yes, it is. We're beginning our Christmas celebration in earnest. I'm going to meet Izzy in the city for lunch today. And – I've decided to take off Saturday, after all!"

Both boys hugged her, and Gabriel jumped up and down while Tommy gave three cheers. As they ate their breakfast the boys listed all the things they were going to see and do.

Lillian was bringing the last of the dishes to the sink, when Tommy jumped out of his seat and ran to the window. "Look! It's snowing!"

Gabriel was at his side in a second. "Mommy! It's snowing!"

Lillian joined them at the window – sure enough, fluffy snowflakes fell from the sky. She couldn't help but connect the snowfall with her change of heart towards the Christmas season.

"So it is! Snow for our first Christmas in Brooklyn. Come, boys! Let's put on your coats and boots."

When they opened the vestibule door, big soft snowflakes drifted from a gray-white sky. Whether it was the snow, the pancakes, or the plans for Saturday, Tommy and Gabriel forgot to complain or roll their eyes or huff in disappointment when they reached the apartment building of the Sisley sisters.

Lillian knocked on their door and soon the twins greeted them. There they were, dressed in identical pale blue dresses with a pattern of sprinkled flowers, and crocheted white cardigans. Lillian quickly looked them over to find what detail was different in their dress. She couldn't immediately detect anything.

"Come in, boys," said one of the twins. "Alice Elizabeth had to cancel her lesson for today, so we have two hours before our first student arrives."

The other twin clapped her hands as if suddenly landing upon a novel idea. "We'll have time to play a few duets for you!"

Tommy and Gabriel politely smiled, and went inside, poking each other. The twins remained standing in the doorway, smiling at Lillian.

Once again, the thought crossed her mind that the sisters knew of her little game. Lillian scanned their attire as they chatted about the coming holiday and the snow, but she couldn't discern any difference between them today – same dress, same brooch, same sweater with scalloped sleeves and hem. Same stockings. Same shoes.

Lillian grew unreasonably frustrated. Try as she might, she couldn't locate the difference. Had they purposely dressed identically today, just to fool her? They could be subtle, Lillian thought, remembering the herringbone stockings. Was it her imagination that their eyes twinkled in merriment?

She couldn't stand there all day, she thought. She would have to give it up. She said her goodbye and began to leave, filled with an absurd sense of defeat.

"Mrs. Hapsey?" said Cynthia. Or perhaps it was Sylvia.

Lillian turned around. "Yes?"

The other sister leaned forward and whispered, "It's the cameos."

"The – " Lillian leaned forward and inspected the gray and white cameos pinned at their collars. Sure enough, one female figure wore a ribbon in her hair.

"So it is," said Lillian. "Thank you! That would have bothered me all day."

As the sisters closed the door, Lillian heard a small chuckle and the words, "We finally stumped her."

Though Lillian was eager to work a few hours on the drawings, she took her time walking back home. She wanted to enjoy the pure white snow. Soon, the superintendents of the various buildings would begin to sprinkle ash from the ash cans onto the sidewalks, turning the snow to pale gray.

She cleared the kitchen table, prepared a cup of tea, and brought her sketch pad and pencils to the table. Her pencil flowed freely as she worked on the scenes that she had begun for Mrs. Cultrain. Other ideas crowded her mind, as if compositions had accumulated inside her over the years, and the floodgates holding them back had burst open. She could have drawn all day – she couldn't remember the last time she had so much energy. She glanced at the clock and set the drawings aside; she would work on them again tonight.

She dressed for her outing in the city, choosing her burgundy tweed suit and a white silk blouse. It seemed perfect for a winter day in the city. She clipped on her pearl earrings, added a bit of lipstick, and checked her reflection. At the last moment, she slipped on her pearl ring with the garnets, fanned out her hand, and smiled. It matched the suit beautifully. She hurried out the door.

On the train ride into Manhattan, she found herself smiling, as if on some great adventure. She quelled her excitement, telling herself she would have to get serious about her new plans and figure out a way to acquire training and experience in office work. She felt both nervous and excited about seeing the offices where Izzy had worked for the past several years. It struck her as odd that she had never been there. Izzy had invited her so many times. Now here she was, finally going. It was all so simple.

She had an hour before meeting Izzy, so she spent it wandering around Rockefeller Center, taking in the Christmas tree, the ice skaters, and gazing up at the skyscrapers. So tall! She realized that she must look like a small-town girl gawking at such wonders. She would always be that small-town girl, but now she was something else as well – exactly what that was, remained to be seen. For the first time in many years, Lillian saw the future as a large and welcoming realm, full of endless paths and possibilities.

Previously, she had watched life from the side, a silent observer. Now she was going to be part of it. She wanted to laugh out loud in delight, and for a moment she again felt like Scrooge – but this time, the transformed Scrooge, after he awoke from the last spirit and threw open the window, asking, "What day is it?" Ecstatic to be alive and to still have a chance at happiness.

She leaned against the railing and looked down at the skaters. Some were inching their way on wobbly feet. Some made progress by hugging the side rails. Others moved ahead with help from friends. There were elegant couples skating in tandem, and several people skating alone, reveling in their independent speed and grace.

Lillian gave a small gasp as one solitary skater fell – and was immediately helped to her feet by a passing skater. They exchanged a few words, laughed, and skated on. There before her and all around, Lillian thought, was life – there was everything she needed to know. She took a last glimpse at the skaters and the tall buildings, and hurried away to find the restaurant where she was meeting Izzy.

She sat at a table to await her friend, and looked out the window, fascinated by the city. The sidewalks were filling up with people on their lunch break – some alone, others with friends or colleagues. Several women held shopping bags filled to the brim. Other people appeared to be tourists, taking pictures and consulting maps.

Again, Lillian felt as if some wand had been waved over her, offering a wider scope of the world, and deepening her understanding of life. She had been asleep before, frozen in place. She would not waste another day, another minute, lamenting the past, fearing Mr. Hinkley or Mrs. Blackham or anyone. There was no time for such foolishness. She must make up for lost time, and begin to –

"Lilly!" Izzy swept down and hugged her. "Gee, I'm glad you're here!" She sat down across from her and asked Lillian how she had spent the morning.

"Mostly gawking like a tourist. But you're right, Izzy. There's something about workday Manhattan that is thrilling. I'm so glad you persuaded me to come."

"I can see you working here, Lilly."

Lillian looked out at the bustling world outside. "Gosh, wouldn't that be exciting!"

"It's all very doable. Once you put your mind to it. I'll help out in any way I can since I would love to have you nearby."

The waiter appeared, greeted them, and handed them menus.

"In the meantime, I'm starving!" said Izzy. "Let's order."

Lillian glanced at the menu, seeing several dishes that were new to her. "So many choices."

"The Paupiettes of Sole with Maine Lobster is delicious. And so is the Breast of Native Guinea Hen."

"Guinea hen," Lillian softly echoed, wondering how similar it was to chicken. "Paupiettes," she said, liking the sound. "I think I'll try that."

"So will I!" Izzy closed her menu and smiled at the waiter who took their order. "And let's start with a glass of champagne. This is a celebration, after all."

The two friends were soon clicking their glasses and filling each other in on their plans for the holidays and updates on their jobs.

Izzy leaned forward and folded her elbows on the table. "Just think, Lilly, if you worked in the city we could meet like this more often." She took another sip of her champagne. "Now tell me more about this drawing project. I like the sound of it."

Lillian told Izzy all about Mrs. Cultrain and the drawings she was working on for her. Then she told Izzy about how she had stood up to Mr. Hinkley, for the first time ever, and how good it felt. And how easy it was.

"Good for you. My boss too, has to be put in place now and then. And on rare occasions, Mr. Rockwell himself."

Lillian's eyes widened. "Oh, Izzy, you are brave!"

Izzy shrugged. "It's just a matter of knowing what you're worth and what you're willing to put up with. Once you know that, you learn to put your foot down."

Lillian nodded at the advice, and stored it away for future use. She had no idea about her worth or her boundaries. She had always believed that whatever a boss requested, had to be done. And yet, somehow she'd found the courage to say no to Mr. Hinkley.

Izzy gazed out the window and sighed. "Isn't life just wonderful?"

Lillian smiled at the effervescence that Izzy couldn't contain. The source obviously came from something more than their lunch together. "Red?" Lillian guessed.

Izzy was momentarily surprised, and then laughed at herself. "Is it so apparent?"

"There's no hiding that glow that comes from being in love."

Izzy had several times clasped her wristwatch. Now she lovingly gazed down at it, and held it out for Lillian to see. "From Red. So that I think about him throughout the day."

Lillian took a closer look at the glittering silver watch. "Oh, Izzy, it's lovely!"

"As if I needed a reminder. He's on my mind day and night. When I'm typing up a report, or catching a bus, or brushing my teeth. He's become a part of me."

"You've never talked about anyone like this, Izzy."

"I've never felt like this about anyone. I feel as if I've known him forever. We spend hours talking over things. He's so comfortable to be with – and yet he's wildly exciting. He does something to me. I'd marry him now, if he asked me."

Lillian leaned back in shock. "You're not serious! You've never been impulsive. You're always so circumspect, always weighing – "

"I can't believe it either, Lilly. Sometimes life surprises us. Shows us a side we didn't know was there."

"That's true," Lillian said, thinking of her own recent changes.

Izzy leaned back as their dishes were placed before them, and Lillian examined the arrangement of sole and vegetables on her plate.

"Look at that! Why, it's a little work of art." She raised her glass again to Izzy, and then tasted her dish. She closed her eyes as the sole melted in her mouth. "Delicious!"

Izzy smiled and took a bite of her meal, but her mind was clearly elsewhere.

"Red's a level-headed guy," she continued. "I don't think he would rush into anything. But you never know."

"Izzy, I can't help wondering – why were you so abrupt with Red the night you met him? I was never more surprised. Except for when he walked back to you."

Izzy's face softened, and she gave a wistful smile. "If he hadn't come to me, I would have had to go to him."

"Why?"

Izzy took a sip of her champagne and narrowed her eyes in thought. "It was like we recognized each other and had no choice but to submit. I knew I would love him. In a way that would undo me. When I first saw him, I thought he was too good to be true. I didn't want him to be perfect. Maybe that's why I snapped at him. And yet he responded with such dignity, didn't he?" Izzy smiled at the memory. "And look at me now. The more I see of him the more I love him."

"I'm happy for you, Izzy. It does seem like you have a lot in common. Including your views on the war."

Izzy's happiness dropped from her face, replaced by concern. "That's the one thing that worries me. He feels so strongly about defending Europe, that he's ready to go and fight. It may be the right thing to do, but I don't want him to go."

"Perhaps it won't come to that."

Izzy remained doubtful. "Red works at his family's construction business. They want him to take it over. He was studying management, but now he's taking classes in aviation and navigation.

I don't think there's any stopping him." She picked up her fork. "I can't even think about it."

The silence was heavy for a moment. Then Izzy shifted the conversation to how Lillian might gain some office experience, and the skills that she believed were most valuable.

They were soon heading to Izzy's workplace for a quick walk-through.

Following Izzy's brisk manner, Lillian pushed through the revolving doors and entered the lobby of Rockwell Publishing. Part of her felt like a fraud, as if she were pretending to be like these other women, so sure of themselves, so smartly dressed, so bold!

Izzy took Lillian to two different floors, pointing out all the job positions for women – secretaries, typists, receptionists, file clerks, and switchboard operators.

Lillian quietly observed the women working. Now and then she asked Izzy a few questions about how long the women had worked there, how they had obtained their experience, and whether they had ever been promoted.

"Come. There's one more floor I want you to see." They rode the elevator up a few floors and entered the Art Department.

Lillian's eyes grew wide, and she stopped just outside the door, unsure about walking into the mostly male department.

Izzy pulled her inside and introduced her to a few people. As on the other floors, everyone seemed to be on friendly terms with Izzy, which put Lillian at ease.

"There are a few lady artists, as you can see. And one or two managers. Would you fancy working here?"

"Now we're really dreaming," Lillian said with a laugh.

"If you're going to dream, dream big." Izzy motioned for her to look at some of the projects the artists were working on.

Lillian watched in awe as one woman put the final touches on a large canvas – a poster-sized advertisement for a face cream. Her eyes became wider as she overheard an older woman request some changes on a drawing made by a man.

"She's one of the senior artists," Izzy whispered.

They exited the Art Department and caught the elevator back to the lobby.

"I have to say, I'm stunned!" said Lillian. "I had no idea such things went on in these buildings."

"But isn't it the same thing you're doing for Mrs. Cultrain? On a smaller scale?"

Lillian looked at Izzy in surprise. "I suppose you're right, Izzy." The doors opened onto the lobby. "Not that I would ever dream of obtaining such a position, but how wonderful it would feel just to be near such a department. How exciting! Oh, Izzy, thank you for showing me all this. I truly am inspired!"

"I knew you would love it. It suits you somehow. I can see you living and working in the city,

Lilly. And meeting me for lunch." She glanced at her watch. "Better be going. As senior typist, I have to make sure the others stay on schedule."

Lillian hugged her friend goodbye. "Thank you, Izzy." She began to leave, then spun around. "Say hello to Red for me."

Izzy clutched her heart and took another glance at her watch. "Four more hours."

Lillian waved goodbye and left the building, happy to see that the snow had begun to fall again. She looked from one tall building to another, thinking that with so many offices, she could surely find work in one of them. And perhaps one job would lead to another. At the department store the most she could ever hope to be was a manager, a prospect that left her uninspired.

She crossed over to Fifth Avenue and walked down the busy sidewalk, dazzled by the constant movement and energy of the city. Most of the department store windows were already decorated for Christmas, but a few were still being draped in lights and decorations. The excitement of the holidays was palpable, and Lillian found herself enjoying the rush and swirl of the season.

She had been to the city many times, but mostly on the weekends, and never in this exuberant frame of mind. The softly falling snow was slowly accumulating on the awnings and tree limbs, outlining everything in white, and adding to the sense of it being Christmastime.

Lillian stopped to admire a candy store, glittering with tinsel and garlands and ornaments. The window displayed beautiful tins of chocolates and golden boxes of candies and miniature marzipan fruits. Among the sweets, several wooden nutcrackers – red, gold, blue, and green – stood sentinel.

Her heart lifted as she suddenly remembered the Christmas that her parents took her and Annette to see the *Nutcracker Suite*. She had fallen in love with the story and the music, and was further transported by the surprise gifts awaiting her and Annette at home – two handsome nutcracker figures – hers blue and Annette's red. They had named them Ludwig and Wolfgang and set them on the mantel every Christmas.

Lillian opened the door, and uttered a soft "Oh!" as she clasped her hands together. The air shimmered with silvery notes coming from a large, upright Victorian music box. She walked closer to it and watched the disc as it slowly rotated, filling the air with a delicate, glittering melody.

She took her time strolling around the little shop – it was a true Christmas fairyland! She would bring Tommy and Gabriel here on one of their trips into the city – they would love it so. After carefully looking at all the choices, she purchased six hooked candy canes for their Christmas tree, a small bag of colorful swirled hard candy, and six chocolate mice for Tommy and Gabriel. Her heart swelled in anticipation at giving them to the boys.

Even though the afternoon was drawing to a close, Lillian continued to walk down the avenue, admiring the window decorations. Just when she decided that it was time to catch the subway home, she looked down a side street, and stopped. Hanging over a shop was a beautifully painted sign for art supplies. She walked down to the store and admired the Christmas window display. It seemed that the day was urging her towards her dreams.

Lillian walked through the store, examining the various materials and observing the other shoppers. A few young art students stood before a shelf of books, discussing the methods of different artists. A striking woman in a long velvet coat inspected small mosaic tiles, holding them up to the light. An older man with paint smudges on his hands inspected panels of wood. A smile crept to Lillian's lips – in their faces she recognized the passion and desire to create.

She meandered from aisle to aisle, lifting oil pastels and pencils, opening sketch pads and running her fingers over the texture of the paper. She felt incredibly rich – all the materials called out to her to be explored, handled, and shaped.

She looked at the boxes of crayons, the tubes of paint, the wooden palettes, and assortment of paint brushes. She paused in front of a magnificent easel, with compartments for a water cup and brushes. She imagined herself standing in front of it, palette in hand, while she painted – alongside a lake? No, a river, with tall leafy trees – she wore a straw hat and her blue smock ruffled in the breeze – she lifted her brush and mixed a bit of celadon green with cerulean blue –

"Looking for a gift?"

Lillian jumped in surprise. A small man with a white goatee smiled kindly, almost as if he approved of her painting among the trees along the river.

"Well, no, I was actually going to buy some supplies for myself."

"Ah, you're an artist then?" he asked, with eyes twinkling.

"I was. I mean, yes, I – I am. Though I have been away from it for a long time."

"But it never leaves you, does it?" He gestured to the woman behind the front counter. "My wife and I have been painting since before we were married – and that was over fifty years ago." He gave a small nod, and then left to help a customer who was looking at sheets of gold leaf.

Lillian could have browsed for hours and hours. Instead, she made a few careful choices – an all-purpose sketch pad and a small tin of brightly colored oil pastels. She could use them for the drawings for Mrs. Cultrain.

At the counter, she spoke briefly with the man and his wife, thanked them, and left the store. She was surprised to find that the day was growing dark.

She cut through a small park on her way to the subway station and took a moment to take in the beauty around her. It was the time of day that most moved her – magical, mystical blue-tinged dusk, the cusp of evening.

The street lamps in the park began to glow brighter against the deepening gray sky. Large, soft snowflakes filled the air. All around her was the rush-hour thrill, everyone in a hurry to go somewhere. The day done, a time when people looked forward to being home, seeing family, a meal around the table. Or perhaps some of them, like Izzy, were going to meet someone special for dinner.

Lillian stood in the park and raised her face towards the sky, to the bare limbs of the tree-tops that were being covered with snow. Then she turned, and gave a little gasp – there, in the distance, nestled between other tall buildings, was the Empire State Building! The sight of it always gave her a thrill. In all the office buildings, soft golden lights lit the windows, giving a sense of warmth and end-of-day activity. Lillian imagined herself working in one of them. She wanted to be part of all this excitement and urgency, this sense of promise that the city held.

Then she smiled. She realized that she was a part of it. An immense sense of gratitude filled her. Everything felt right. And in that moment, there was an acceptance – an embrace, even – of who she was, of how she took in the world and communicated with it.

"I am dream driven," she said to herself. "There's no sense fighting it."

She clutched her bags of art supplies and candies, and entered the subway station. On the ride home, she planned the evening for her boys. She knew exactly what she would do, and she would have just enough time.

She stopped at the Christmas tree lot and bought a pine garland, a bunch of holly, and a wreath. Weighted down with all her treasures, she hurried home to decorate the apartment.

First, she placed a few sprigs of holly on the wreath, added a red ribbon to it, and hung it on her apartment door. Next, she cleared the top of the bookcase and draped the pine bough over it to serve as their mantelpiece. From the back of the cupboard, she dug out all the Christmas decorations she could find, including her old nutcracker prince. She set them among the greenery, along with a few candles.

Then, she moved the table by her bedside into the living room and set it against the wall. She lifted the small Christmas tree and set it on top, took a step back, and smiled. Much better. She fixed a small star on top of the tree, and then plugged in the lights – magical! She would let Tommy and Gabriel hang the ornaments. Under the tree she set a small quilt with the red calico backing turned up.

She rummaged through the box of decorations and took out the tinsel. She draped several strands on the tree, making it sparkle and come to life. Inspired by the effect, she decided to hang tinsel all around the apartment, something she had never done. The apartment became her canvas. She draped tinsel from the picture frames and mirror, from the lampshades and bookshelves, until the room itself began to shimmer.

Lastly, she gathered the collection of glass ornaments and the boxes of candy and placed them beneath the tree. She stood by the door to take it all in. The room looked beautiful!

She turned on a single lamp and unplugged the tree lights. Before Tommy and Gabriel entered, she would plug them in and light a few candles.

Lillian walked the two blocks to the Sisley sisters and was soon walking home with Tommy and Gabriel. When she turned a corner instead of going straight towards the apartment, the boys stopped and looked at each other. "Where're you going, Mommy?"

"I thought we'd have dinner at Saporito's."

Tommy and Gabriel cheered in happiness and ran to take her hands.

Over dinner Tommy and Gabriel wriggled in happiness and talked about whatever came to their minds. They told her about the last piano student who missed all the notes, and the Christmas cookies the Sisley sisters gave them. They asked her about the Christmas tree in Rockefeller Center, and the decorations on Fifth Avenue. Gabriel asked, "Does elf rhyme with shelf?" and Tommy talked about how Dom and Tony were going to let him operate the train. Lillian reached over and took their hands. "My happiness," she said, causing their smiles to widen.

On arriving home, the boys ran upstairs. "A wreath!" they both called out, reaching up to touch it.

"Wait here for just a moment." Lillian entered the apartment and closed the door behind her.

Tommy and Gabriel stood in the hall, look-ing at each other in perplexity.

"Why?" Tommy called through the door. "Can't we come in?"

"What are you doing, Mommy?" added Gabriel.

Lillian plugged in the Christmas tree lights and lit the candles on the bookshelf and in front of the mirror, doubling the points of lights. She ran over and opened the door.

Tommy and Gabriel stepped inside, stopped, and gaped.

"Christmas!" whispered Gabriel.

Tommy twisted out of his coat, his eyes wide. "Wow! How'd you do this, Mommy?" His eyes traveled to the bookcase, the candles, the glittering tinsel, and finally rested on the Christmas tree. "You got a new tree?"

"No, I just lifted it up a bit. I thought we could decorate the tree this evening. I set the boxes of ornaments next to it." The boys ran to the tree, touching it affectionately and unable to stop smiling.

"Take a look in the little boxes next to the ornaments," Lillian said.

Tommy and Gabriel each opened a box.

"Candy canes!" cried Tommy. "And Christmas candy!" He leaned closer to inspect the brightly colored candies.

Gabriel lifted the paper from the smaller box and almost choked in excitement. "Chocolate mice! Look, Tommy." He ran and hugged Lillian. "I love chocolate mice!"

*

After an evening of decorating the tree, listening to Christmas music on the radio, and sipping hot chocolate while they finished *A Christmas Carol*, Lillian tucked the boys into bed.

She felt that she was stepping into a new future, one filled with excitement and warmth and happiness. She realized that life was ever-changing, full of surprises and awakenings.

On the kitchen table, she spread out the drawings for Mrs. Cultrain and set the bag from the art store next to them. Then, almost as if it were a ceremony, she gently lifted out the materials. She opened the new sketch pad and looked at the white page, full of possibilities. One by one, she took out the oil crayons and drew a few flourishes of color, delighting in the vibrant hues, the smooth texture, even the names of the colors.

She imagined herself going to work in Manhattan, stylishly dressed, with a portfolio under her arm – and laughed at the boldness of her vision. Then she selected a few jewel-toned crayons and added some color to the drawings.

Chapter 10

Christmas was now just a week away, and Lillian was almost sad that the season was passing by so quickly. She had rekindled her excitement for Christmastime. Nothing momentous had taken place, and yet she felt that her life had changed.

The little Christmas tree in the apartment was perfect – especially now that several presents lay wrapped beneath it. While browsing for gifts for Tommy and Gabriel, she had come across some Western-themed flannel pajamas with cowboys twirling lassos above their heads, a few bucking broncos, a campfire scene with two guitar-playing cowboys. She purchased the blue set for Gabriel and the red for Tommy. She was sure they would love them. Also wrapped were board games, Tinker Toys for Gabriel, a model airplane kit for Tommy, and a few comic books and boxes of crayons.

She had enjoyed the "Christmas Night" event at the department store, even though she had to work. Izzy and Red had stopped by, before going out to dinner – if anything, they were even more in love. All in all, it had been a wonderful evening – even Mr. Hinkley was in the holiday spirit. He had hired a new sales clerk, another pretty girl like Letitia, but this one had an air of authority that Lillian thought would serve the girl well. She had ambition and wasn't cowed by Mr. Hinkley.

Most of all, Lillian had been elated to hear that the drawings for the Housewares Department had been a huge success, and that most of the items featured in the drawings had sold out. Housewares won the "best-dressed" department for the holidays, which thrilled Mrs. Cultrain. Lillian felt that the first step in her new journey had been taken. Not only had she earned a little extra money, but the experience had given her an enormous sense of satisfaction.

A few days later, Mrs. Cultrain saw Lillian in the lunchroom and pulled up a chair next to her. She thanked her again for the success of the drawings.

In spite of the cheerful words, Lillian picked up on her subdued manner. "Is anything wrong, Mrs. Cultrain?"

"No, but I'm afraid I won't be here much longer. My husband is being relocated to Chicago. It's a good opportunity for him – too good to pass up. So, … "

"So, you'll be leaving." Lillian couldn't hide her disappointment. She had envisioned other campaigns with Mrs. Cultrain. She had so enjoyed their meetings and discussions.

Mrs. Cultrain nodded. "There will be plenty of opportunities there for me – though it will take me a while to get settled in. A new home, new schools. Chances are it will be a good year before I can even think about taking a position." She straightened her shoulders. "That will give me a chance to look around. See what the possibilities are. I'm up to the challenge."

"I'm sure you'll make the most of it," said Lillian, with no doubt that Mrs. Cultrain would find success.

"Listen. Why don't you think about moving to a different department? I could put in a word for you, if you wanted."

"Thank you, Mrs. Cultrain. But you've made me realize something about myself, and the dreams I thought I had given up on. I'm not sure how I'm going to do it, but I've decided to pursue my art, and find a better paying job."

"I'm glad to hear it! Nothing is sadder than the death of a dream."

Though Lillian was disappointed that Mrs. Cultrain was leaving, in her heart, she knew that she herself wouldn't be in Brooklyn, let alone the department store, for much longer. She had made a promise to herself that by the end of the following year she would be living and working in Manhattan.

*

On the day of Mrs. Rossi's party, Lillian awoke with the comfort of a pleasant dream still nestled in her mind. She lay in bed a few moments longer, trying to remember the sweet dream. She closed her eyes, hoping the images would reappear. What was the feeling? Deep happiness? A mix of peace and excitement? Calm and passion? She decided it must be all the new emotions surging through her, the new-found sense of hope, the rediscovery of her touchstone.

She sat up in bed, eager to begin the day – but was overcome with a sense of loss that the dream was over. *I'm being absurd. It's just a dream.* She waited a few moments, waiting for the feeling to pass. It was surprisingly persistent, tugging at her. Whatever the emotion the dream had stirred up, she wanted more of it. She didn't want to let it go. She lay down again and closed her eyes. Surely, if she tried, she could recall one image that would trigger the rest of the dream. She took a deep breath and slowly let it out – and waited.

"Mommy! Can I have cereal?" Gabriel's voice coming from the kitchen spurred her to action.

She threw back the covers. "Coming!"

Though she thought she had shrugged off the dream, it stayed with her all day. It lingered when she took the boys to the Sisley sisters, when she rang up sales in the dress salon, when she sketched over her lunch break, and when she caught the trolley home in the falling snow.

It was like being haunted by a sweetness – a little glittery cloud of enchantment that hovered around her and made her happy. Perhaps it simply meant that her future had brightened, that it was now a welcoming place.

While she and the boys dressed for the party, Tommy and Gabriel guessed at their presents under the tree, squeezing and shaking the wrapped boxes. They had eaten four chocolate mice and were saving the last two for Christmas Eve.

Lillian decided to wear her floral crepe dress that always reminded her of a garden. Though it was part of her work wardrobe, she would dress it up with her deep blue velvet shawl. She clipped on gold drop earrings, and added a touch of lipstick and dab of powder.

"Come on, boys. Put on your coats." She lifted the platter of gingerbread cake she had made the night before along with a container of caramel sauce and set them by the door. She held Gabriel's coat open while he put his arms through the sleeves, and then buttoned it up for him. After adjusting her hat in the mirror, she slipped on her coat.

"This is a happy Christmas!" Gabriel announced. "Right, Taffy?" he asked, setting the teddy bear in the armchair. "Right, Tommy?"

Lillian's heart swelled at the words and she waited to hear Tommy's response.

Tommy looked up at her as he pulled on his coat. "The best Christmas ever!"

The snow continued to fall as they walked the two blocks to the Rossi's. Wreaths hung on doors, pine boughs were twined around railings, and several windows showed Christmas trees with lights and twinkling ornaments. It seemed that Christmas was everywhere they looked.

When the door opened to the Rossi's apartment, Lillian caught the aromas of garlic and onions, herbs and butter. Suddenly, she was very hungry.

"Come in, come in," said Mr. Rossi. "I know what these boys like to eat. Eh, Tommy?" He put an arm around Tommy and Gabriel and led them to the dining room. "And Gabriel, we have plenty of sweets for you."

Mrs. Rossi took Lillian by the arm and followed, introducing her to people on the way, including her sister Vera and her husband. They were obviously deeply in love, which reminded Lillian of Izzy and Red.

Lillian and the boys were handed plates and Mrs. and Mr. Rossi insisted that they try a little bit of everything. The array of foods was spectacular. Lillian tried to remember the names of the items being piled on her plate.

"This is *spiedini*, my favorite," said Mr. Rossi.

"And you must try this," said Mrs. Rossi. "It's my mother's *braciola* – one of her specialties."

Mr. Rossi added olives and cheese and bread to their plates. "Make sure you get some of these *arancini*. What can I get you to drink?" He waved his arm to the counter where glasses and various drinks were set out.

Tommy and Gabriel were soon pulled away by Dominic, Tony, and Mary, while Lillian made her way to an empty chair next to a group of women. When someone began to play a song on the piano,

Mr. Rossi took his wife by the arm and began to dance with her.

The rooms grew increasingly crowded and noisy, full of good food and much laughter. Children ran around from room to room in games of their own. At one point, Gabriel ran up holding hands with little Mary. "This is just like the Fezziwig's, Mommy," he shouted, and then ran off.

Lillian could understand why Tommy and Gabriel liked to be over here and why they were so taken with Vera. She was a jewel – lively and warm, and she was a natural with children. All the kids crowded around her, vying for her attention.

"Watch me!" they cried, standing in front of her. "Look what I can do!" they said, demonstrating some talent like hopping on one foot, holding their breath, making animal sounds, or, in Gabriel's case, rhyming words.

Lillian was enjoying the singing from the group gathered around the piano, when she saw Mrs. Rossi and Vera coming towards her.

"Do you have everything you need?" asked Mrs. Rossi.

"More than enough," Lillian laughed, gesturing to her plate. "This has been just wonderful for me and the boys. I'm so happy that you'll be close by, Vera."

"We were just saying the same thing." Mrs. Rossi exchanged a look with her sister. "I hope you don't think I'm intruding, but I was mentioning to Vera that you were having a hard time finding a babysitter, and she had a wonderful idea." She nudged her sister. "Go on, tell her!"

"Well, if you would like, I was thinking that perhaps I could watch your boys. We get along well and I'm close by now."

Lillian's eyes widened. "Why, that would be marvelous! But are you sure?"

"Completely sure. At least for the next year or so."

Mrs. Rossi leaned in, and added, "She's hoping for one of her own, you know."

"But until then, I'm available, if you like."

"Your offer couldn't come at a better time. Oh, I can hardly wait to tell Tommy and Gabriel."

A request for more punch was made by one of the guests, and soon Lillian and Vera were filling punch glasses while Mrs. Rossi made another batch.

After a few hours, Lillian took her leave, flushed with the sense of goodwill and merrymaking – and delighted that Vera had solved one of her biggest problems.

Mrs. Rossi wouldn't let her leave without packing a small box of desserts. Music and laughter followed Lillian and the boys down the stairs to the vestibule door. Outside, they emerged into a soft, quiet world, white with fresh snow. Lillian took a deep breath and lifted her face in happiness. The walk home in the cold air amid the peacefulness of the night was the perfect way to end a wonderful evening.

Lillian decided it was the perfect time to tell them who their new babysitter would be. They jumped up and down, crying "Hooray!" She walked behind boys, smiling. Their arms were around each other's shoulders as they chatted about the party.

As they crossed the street, Lillian noticed a man and woman walking ahead of them. The man lovingly drew the young woman closer, and they nestled their heads together.

Lillian stopped suddenly – and stared. A shudder jolted through her as the details of her dream from the morning flashed before her. She remained rooted to the spot, startled to remember that it had been a dream of love. She had been passionately in love. In a deeply-rooted relationship. The details came flooding back – a kind, gentle man had wrapped his arm around her as they walked through a park. They had laughed and kissed.

Lillian cocked her head – had it been Tom? No, it had been an older man. She felt momentarily guilty that it wasn't Tom – though she had no idea who the man was. The strongest feeling was that it had all felt so right. But who was the man?

It was no one, she decided. She shook her head and continued walking. It must be all the talk of Izzy and Red. Or maybe the effects of reading about old Scrooge awaking to life – and her own awakening.

But once again, the strength of the feeling gripped her, the closeness she felt to the man, and the depth of their love. She halted, stunned by the possibility – *Surely that's not in my future? Is there still a chance for love in my life?* Once more, she was suffused by the sense of sweetness and a kind of happiness she had never known.

Tommy and Gabriel realized that she was several steps behind them and ran back to her. "Come on, Mom! Let's hurry back to our Christmas home."

"I'll carry the desserts," said Tommy, taking the box from Lillian.

She smiled and took their hands.

"Can we plug in the Christmas tree lights?" asked Gabriel.

"How about we have some hot chocolate to warm up?" said Tommy.

"Can we open one of our stocking presents?"

To each question, Lillian, half enveloped in her dream, answered *yes*, causing Tommy and Gabriel's eyes to widen in increasing excitement.

Lillian smiled down at her boys, and at the Christmas lights in the windows, and out at the softly falling snow – and wondered at the sweet mystery of life.

Made in the USA
Coppell, TX
30 November 2019